JOHN COON

Feral Lands

Samak Press

First published by Samak Press 2025

Copyright © 2025 by John Coon

This novel is entirely a work of fiction. The names, characters and incidents portrayed in it are the work of the author's imagination. Any resemblance to actual persons, living or dead, events or localities is entirely coincidental.

Individual story copyrights: The House on Europa ©2025 Frances Addison. Scratcher ©2025 John Coon. Edge Mountain Hello ©2025 R.E. Dyer. Containment Protocols ©2025 Aaron Frale. The Angora Incident ©2025 Mark Gardner. Holes ©2025 Michael Paige. Anticipating Ruins ©2025 Lucretia Stanhope. The Thorny One of the Water ©2025 Mike Sullivan.

First edition

ISBN: 979-8-99-113422-4

Editing by John Coon

This book was professionally typeset on Reedsy.
Find out more at reedsy.com

"If you gaze long enough into an abyss,
the abyss will gaze back into you."

— FRIEDRICH NIETZSCHE

Contents

I

The House on Europa

By: Frances Addison

The House on Europa

The house had absolutely no business being there.

That didn't stop it from being in a place it shouldn't be, of course, but Jemma thought it was an important fact to acknowledge. Fastidious to a fault and a scientist through and through, she'd already assembled a mental list of reasons why the house simply couldn't be there. Any single point offered persuasive enough evidence on its own. The list was as follows:

Firstly, the structure didn't appear to have been *built*. No bricks. No mortar. Though hard to tell at a glance, the entire thing appeared to be constructed from perfectly moulded, continuous stone. A carving was the only reasonable explanation, but Jemma hadn't found a single chisel mark on the entire exterior.

Perhaps more damningly, the house was obviously modeled after her childhood home, shuttered windows and all. The only differences were a lack of any doors and glass in the windows, and the aforementioned stony facade in place of the burnt umber bricks she'd once loved. Unusual for a great many reasons, not the least being that said childhood home had burned down nearly twenty years ago.

The stone itself was gray-green, not dissimilar in visual composition to granite. Likely igneous, but impossible to identify without further study. Though Jemma couldn't identify any obvious source of heat, the house emitted enough warmth to melt a circle in the surrounding ice, uncovering more of the same alien rock.

The last reason on her list also happened to be the conundrum that intrigued her most: No one could possibly have built — or even carved — the house because only ten people in the history of humanity had ever set foot on Europa before and not one of those visitors had ever mentioned anything about a construction project. It wasn't the sort of thing astronauts tended to leave out of their reports.

A multitude of other reasons could surely be found for why a distinctly European house shouldn't be quietly existing on a Jovian moon four hundred million miles from where it was supposed to be, but those seemed like the most pressing matters. Jemma would probably be able to dig deeper when her brain wasn't busy tripping over itself in utter bafflement.

She wasn't even really scared, though distantly aware she probably should be. In the depths of her mind, some primitive instinct that once kept her ancient ancestors alive screamed at her that something was wrong with this situation. Still, mere survival instinct wasn't strong enough to overwhelm her curiosity. She was too many generations removed from those early hominids, too many millennia deep in investing in higher brain functions for their life-saving inheritance to pay off now. Humanity had grown smart enough to reach for the stars themselves and lost so much more than they would ever know in the process.

Jemma finished her loose loop around the structure in front of the main 'door'. It loomed as a vacant hole in the side of the wall, perfectly proportioned to allow her to pass through even while wearing her bulky EVA suit. All around her, the whisper thin freeze of Europa's tenuous atmosphere fluttered with fine motes of dust, drifting ceaselessly in total silence. The only audible sounds were her own rasping breaths and the heavy, hard thumping of her heart. Above, a sky overflowing with stars wheeled ever onwards.

She knew she shouldn't cross the threshold before her. Her very bones were sang against the wrongness of what she'd found, warning that she didn't need to understand how the house got there to know she shouldn't want any part in it.

Except... If it wasn't built by a human — and it definitely hadn't been — then logic dictated *something else* built it.

They'd come here in the first place to search for life. Her fellow astronauts thought they might find it in vast oceans locked beneath the ice at her feet, but the universe was tricky. The space race of the fifties and sixties had put humanity on the moon and given them non-stick frying pans in the process; sometimes looking for one thing helped you uncover something else along the way.

Maybe their search for life beneath Europa's icy crust was really just a steppingstone to finding life *on* the ice instead.

The one admission she gave to her training was to key her radio before she stepped closer. It hissed with static, an aggressive buzz distinctly different from the quiet hum it should have been if the line had been clear and functional.

"Asterius Lander, this is Specialist Lockley. I've found — something. Some sort of stone structure. I'm going to check it out, over."

More hissing static.

"Asterius, do you copy?"

She double checked the panel on her wrist, but it didn't display anything out of the ordinary. All her vital signs were within normal limits and her oxygen supply was still a good 80% full. It didn't indicate she'd lost connection to the landing module.

That really should have been the final sign that she was interfering with something she should leave alone. If anything, though, it buoyed Jemma's spirits. She was human, fallible. The suit was a mesh of metal and wires and programming. It couldn't be wrong. Thousands of dollars and decades of human innovation had been poured into it her equipment to ensure it would not fail, no matter the circumstances. If the suit said all was well, then it wasn't lying.

"Asterius, do you read me?"

Still no reply. Jemma didn't think she'd strayed too far — her oxygen would be running lower if she had — but the featureless, blank canyons of ice and rock provided few reliable landmarks to judge her position. Maybe she'd stumbled into a strange magnetic field, and it wasn't letting her signal through.

Proper procedure dictated she should retreat until she regained a signal. Base instinct told her she should run as far and as fast as she could from the house. Common sense told her she was playing with fire.

She ignored logic and emotion alike, and stepped through the doorway.

The inside of the house was as familiar as the outside. Just as in her memory, the hall stretched out in front of her, bordered on either side by doors that once led to the kitchen and the dining room. Ahead and to the left stood the staircase, a perfect replication down to the slanted third step that had tripped up every single guest that had ever visited. Her mother had always been mad that Dad never found the time to fix it.

If Jemma had needed any further evidence the house shouldn't be here, she was staring right at it. That broken stair burned to ashes decades ago. Both of her parents were ten years gone themselves. Jemma doubted any human alive, other than herself, remembered that step's existence. Yet there it was, in perfect 96° form.

As if someone had crafted it for her and her alone.

"Hello?"

She called out without thinking. No response would reach her. Even if the mysterious, impossible builder was still in here, her suit trapped any noises she made, and the atmosphere was far too thin to carry her voice even if she turned on her external radio. She was isolated in the truest sense. Without the suit, she'd last no more than mere seconds. With it, she was completely disconnected from everything around her.

Sealed away.

Trapped.

Her feet carried her forwards without conscious thought. The house was curiously devoid of furniture. Walls and doorways were all where they were supposed to be, but the ephemera she remembered being scattered across counter tops and spilling off shelves was all absent. It reminded her morbidly of a sun-bleached whale carcass washed up on shore after all the seabirds had taken their fill. Stripped bare bones were all that remained of the house, a skeleton bereft of meaning and life. That, more than its placement, more than its sheer, vast *aloneness*, was the first thing that made Jemma think *lonely*.

That wasn't to say the house wasn't without some comforts. For starters, it was far warmer in the house than should be possible — her suit registered a balmy -50° C — but that still didn't account for all the melted ice outside. The melting point of water should technically have *increased* in lower atmospheric pressure, and here it was liquefying at a much lower temperature than should have been possible. In the grand scheme of the mystery she'd stumbled across, it wasn't high on her list of concerns. Nonetheless, she dutifully added it to the bottom.

God, when she made it back to the Asterius, no one was going to believe her.

Abruptly, the idea that she might be hallucinating crossed her mind. Jemma wouldn't be the first person to feel the tug of madness among planets and moons humans had never been designed for. And yet it didn't feel like a hallucination. When she reached out to press her hand to the wall beside her, a spot where a photo of her parents had once hung, it pushed back against her palm as solidly as any building she'd ever touched. She half-thought she could feel a distinct warmth of it on her palm, but that had to be her imagination. Her EVA suit guarded against all forms of radiation.

Climbing the stairs was no easy feat in all her gear, so she took it at a snail's pace. She admired the walls as she climbed, her memory flaring to drop in the colour of the wallpaper she'd once known, the frames housing pictures that had lined the ascent, the scuff mark halfway down from where her uncle had once tripped and fallen. If stairs creaked beneath her now like the ones in her memory, she would never know.

The house grew colder upstairs. Darker, somehow. It didn't make any real sense — she'd been operating mostly by torchlight since the sun's illumination was little better than Earth's moonlight so far from the system's centre — but she noted the difference all the same.

The recreation's subtle details faltered here as well. The landing should have revealed three doorways: the bathroom and the two bedrooms. Instead, walls flowed in solid sheets from floor to ceiling, broken only by three faint indents that marked the spots where door frames used to be. As if rooms still lay beyond but had been sealed away from her.

Or, perhaps, as if construction hadn't yet finished.

As if more still needed to be done.

The strange sense of welcome that had lured her up here drained away in one sudden swoop, even as a creeping coldness seeped over Jemma's entire body. She froze on the top step, her torch beam quivering faintly over the spot that should have led to her parents' bedroom. Her breathing sped up.

This was *wrong*.

It had always been wrong, right from the start.

What was she *doing* here?

Icy terror locked down hard around her lungs, punching a sound from her chest more suited to a wounded animal. She recognised it as her own voice only because she felt the way it burned on the way out, stealing whatever lingering bravery she had left. She couldn't move. When she tried to turn and run, her body simply didn't obey. It refused. Every muscle in her was tense and helpless.

Humans had lived at the top of their respective food chains for so long, they'd forgotten what it felt like to be *prey*. Jemma's body relearned it in an instant.

A low rumble beneath her feet shook her immobile limbs. The tremors were faint enough that, for a moment, she mistook them for her own hopeless quaking. Then her torch revealed movement ahead and an entirely new fear gripped her. Frozen, Jemma was forced to watch as unblemished rock hiding her parents' bedroom rippled and began to crack apart, splitting in two as a fissure opened up right through its centre. The movement ebbed and flowed in sporadic, rhythmic bursts, the cavity almost pulsing as it split wider and wider.

Like the beat of a heart.

Like something *living*.

For just a second, Jemma feared she'd either vomit or faint as a dizzying cocktail of terror overrode all self-control, before her hind brain finally, *finally* kicked into gear. Adrenaline dumped into her bloodstream like battery acid, burning and bubbling and providing exactly the kick she needed to unstick her feet from the floor. Finally, Jemma did what she should have done ten minutes ago: turn and flee.

She had no idea if the crack in the wall continued to grow or not, but she was long past caring. Only fleeing mattered to her now. All higher considerations faltered and died. Survival was all there was.

Jemma's attempts at flight were immediately thwarted. EVA suits were not designed with running in mind. Europa's feeble gravity was the only reason Jemma didn't trip and fall her way down the stairs. Even when her footfalls were out of place and she missed a step, she still had ample time to catch herself and keep moving without cartwheeling down the stairs to her miserable, lonely death. It saved her, but it also meant navigating a ten-second line to the door took almost thirty.

Each added second was agonising. Every breath whined in and out of her chest, a sound of primal terror, and her pounding heart threatened to break through her ribs. Distantly, her suit started to chirp with alarm at her rapidly degrading stats. She paid it no mind. Jemma faced a far greater danger here than running down her oxygen supply a little faster than normal.

Making it through the front door again was a victory all on its own, the star-filled ink of the sky rushing over her head in one sudden swell of black. When she'd first arrived on Europa, the sky's emptiness had left her feeling exposed; now, it was a blessing.

It meant she was *out*.

That didn't stop her running, of course. Jemma had no intention of stopping until she reached the Asterius. Europa had other ideas. The second she cleared the defrosted stone circle, a hidden ice pocket cracked under her left boot and swallowed her foot whole. She staggered to catch herself awkwardly on her one free leg, briefly terrified all over again that she'd torn her suit and equally horrified to realise her escape attempt had been thwarted.

For several long, agonising seconds, Jemma could only stand there and *sob*. Her chest ached with the force of terror she'd been trying to contain, so painful that she couldn't even bring herself to look down at her trapped foot even as desperate seconds ticked away. Turning to look back at the house was a complete impossibility.

Slowly, she brought her breathing back under control. It was uneven and uncomfortable, but the shot of adrenaline that first got her moving was fading and, in its absence, her higher brain functions began to reassert dominance. It was basic training in the end, one of the first things she'd ever been taught: prioritise.

What's the first thing that might kill you?

An impossible question to answer when she had no solid evidence if anything inside the house truly wanted to hurt her. That wasn't information she could get obtain without going back inside — not an option — so she had to disregard it. Ignoring the potential threat felt like ignoring that her skin was on fire, but no other option presented itself.

Without any understanding of the house, her next largest threat was shared by all astronauts: exposure. She had a limited amount of oxygen and a limited amount of power to keep her suit working. The readout on her wrist cheerfully reported both factors were within normal limits — a slightly lower than normal O2 stat notwithstanding — but that wouldn't last forever. She had to return to the Asterius soon and that meant freeing her foot.

Pulling gently at the trapped limb did nothing and tugging too harshly might compromise her suit. She'd need to dig it out. Trying not to give herself time to overthink the situation, she dropped to one knee and pulled out the climbing axe affixed to her belt that she'd been given for exactly situations like this one. With extreme care and a single-minded determination that would make any ancient monk proud, she sank the blade into rocky ice and started working herself free.

Beneath her, the ground rumbled.

Jemma moaned in fear. The tremor could have been anything — Europa was known for quakes. No reason why this one couldn't be counted among many natural events she'd already experienced since her arrival.

Her intuition told her otherwise. She didn't know how or why, but she knew the house caused the quake. It matched the one inside. Something was *moving*.

Was it better to look behind her or would looking only make things worse?, In that regard, being in that the EVA suit was a blessing. Bulky and rigidly fixed to the torso section, her helmet didn't allow her to turn more than 45 degrees in either direction. Turning to look back at the house was impossible without reorienting her entire body, and she couldn't do *that* without freeing her foot. It made the decision for her.

Do not look.

That didn't stop her from picturing it. Some figure, maybe, emerging from a secret hideaway now that it had lured her into its trap. Or maybe the entire house was reforming the way the doorway had been, growing into something new. Something unspeakable. Unimaginable. Maybe it was drawing closer.

Tears streamed down her face, turning her lips salty. She couldn't seem to stop shaking.

Then, with a suddenness that startled her, the axe broke through the last sharp jut of ice trapping her foot in place. She tumbled free with a start, nearly ending up sprawled on the ground for her trouble. She caught herself with a bitten off yell and, upon regaining her balance, she skittered across the ground on all fours to put distance between herself and whatever horrors loomed in the dark behind her. She made it as far as a small rocky outcropping that gave her the leverage she needed to get back on her feet and turned.

Nothing.

Nothing was behind her.

The house was gone.

In the beam of her torchlight, idle snow drifted silently through unbroken, empty space. The light reached a small rise some sixty metres away and the space between here and there held no more than Europa's thin air and the darkness of distant stars. Even the ring of melted ice was now absent.

Jemma stared. Horror still balled so high within her throat she couldn't fill her lungs around it. She hadn't imagined the house. She could feel the aftershocks of her terror in still twitching exhausted muscles, could still recall with crystal clarity the wall's solidity beneath her hand. It hadn't been some waking dream. Everything she saw was real. She *knew* it had been real.

"Hello?"

The question left her as a near silent rasp. Her throat was fried. No one was there to hear her anyway. Even without the suit, she was the only living soul for miles around with nothing but ice and dust for company. Her colleagues on the Asterius were over an hour's trek away.

For a few heartbeats, Jemma couldn't decide whether to be glad she seemed to be alone or terrified by her solitude. If whoever — or whatever — had built the house was still out there somewhere... did they watch her even now? It was a long walk back to the lander with nothing but her thoughts for company and no easy way to watch over her shoulder. In all her life, she'd never felt so exposed. So defenceless. The weight of it hung from her bones like a restraint, holding her heavily in place.

Perhaps the house really was a trap only now springing closed.

Or, maybe, it already had.

Ahead, beyond the spot where the house had once stood, the flaming orange might of Jupiter finally crested the horizon and began its silent climb into the sky.

Frances Addison is and avid reader and author across all genres of fiction. She spends her working life writing about video games. When she is not doing any of that, you can probably find her somewhere waxing lyrical about obscure science and mythology to anyone who will listen. Frances resides in the United Kingdom.

II

Scratcher

By: John Coon

Scratcher

Sitting alone before a makeshift fire pit only encouraged old boy scout campfire tales to crawl through Joshua's head like a legion of ants. He stared at yellow flames feasting on a knee-high pile of dry branches while stretching out his aching leg. Recalling scary stories wouldn't bother him so much if he weren't stuck deep in a darkened forest that harbored darker secrets.

A swollen ankle left him in this predicament.

Joshua prepared for multiple worst-case scenarios before setting out on a simple backpacking trip to Dragonfly Lake. Except for one. He rubbed his palms down his forehead and across his nose before letting out an anxious sigh.

Damn. Those long-ago camping trips with his old troop had become his new enemy.

Their scary stories made for convenient urban legends. Older scouts used them as a scare tactic to initiate tenderfoots. His senior patrol leader derived pleasure from seeing all the youngest troop members freak out like scared puppies over every word and random noise. Deer Falls had been ground zero for a plethora of urban legends longer than he'd been alive. Human-eating monsters roaming the forest featured prominently in numerous tales. Still, people who knew better never believed that shit.

Why should he start?

"Get a grip," Joshua mumbled. "You're an adult now. Don't lose your mind over stupid shit from boy scouts."

Losing his footing on a steep trail put him in a tough enough situation. No need to make things worse by dredging up stories buried a decade away from his temporary campsite.

Joshua cast his eyes down on his injured left foot, resting on a flat smooth rock. He scrounged rocks from a nearby creek bed and brought them all back to his campsite a safe distance from the bank. A rough splint, held together with a beige elastic bandage, flanked both sides of Joshua's swollen ankle. Fashioning a workable splint from a fallen tree branch took him half an hour. He sliced the branch into two equal-sized pieces with a folding saw and whittled away bark in fluid strokes with his camping knife until only smooth wood remained.

His homemade splint worked better than expected considering his source materials. It wasn't foolproof though. Any sudden lateral step to his left stung like a hammer driving a nail through solid bone. Still, if he kept the sprained ankle elevated and motionless, the pain receded to more tolerable levels.

Only a bad sprain, Joshua silently assured himself. *It'll heal enough for me to make it back down the rest of the trail tomorrow.*

If his ankle allowed, he planned to depart right after sunrise before cool mountain air yielded to the sun's baking heat. Joshua realized he needed to give himself time to cover enough ground to get help. Far too many miles on the return leg of his seven-mile hike remained ahead of him.

Joshua refocused his gaze on the crackling flames and pulled a thermal blanket tighter around his shoulders. If his parents knew what fate had befallen him, search and rescue teams would swarm Dragonfly Lake and the surrounding area within the hour. They wouldn't rest until he was back in Deer Falls in one piece. Before a previous solo backpacking trip deep into the Arapaho National Forest, his mom insisted he call her and check in when he arrived and then later when he left to go home.

"I'll be fine, Mom." His exasperated response from their recent conversation popped into his head, feeling as fresh as if he said those words only a few minutes earlier. "I know Dragonfly Lake like the back of my hand."

"You really shouldn't go up there alone," she insisted. "Your dad and I worry about you getting lost or hurt on these backpacking trips."

"I'm an experienced hiker. I'm always prepared.

"Why don't you take Jessica along with you? She seems like such a sweet girl."

"Yeah ... Jessica decided she'd rather go fishing in another pond."

An awkward pause and uneasy silence followed his revelation about his ex-girlfriend's infidelity.

"I just don't want anything to happen to you," his mom finally said

"Trust me. You have no reason to worry."

Turned out his parents had valid reasons to worry. Dammit. Why did he insist on taking a panoramic photo? If Joshua had only lowered his camera and turned to survey the terrain behind him before stepping back. Then he could have sidestepped the divot that swallowed his foot and ripped his ankle out from under him.

A mournful howl pierced the silence around the campfire. Joshua's heart began pounding faster and harder. Other howls joined the first. All from deep within a thicket of trees directly southwest of his campsite. The shadowy blanket of night so thoroughly enveloped all surrounding trees that Joshua struggled to make out any movement beyond the flames of his diminutive fire.

He turned his head and cocked his ear toward the howls. Each progressive howl varied from the preceding one, rising and falling in pitch. Staccato yaps punctuated howls here and there. Joshua pinched his eyelids shut and bit down on his lower lip.

Coyotes.

How many?

Sleep would be impossible with coyotes lurking in the nearby woods. Their howls sounded close. Too close.

"That's the scariest part, you know."

Brody's voice popped unbidden into Joshua's head. He never gave his old senior patrol leader a second thought after high school. Now one specific story stuck to his mind like glue.

"The scratcher can mimic all sorts of wild animals." Brody held a flashlight under his chin for dramatic effect. "One minute you think you're hearing a wolf or a coyote or maybe even an owl. The next minute, you're dinner."

Other scouts sat on a fallen log on either side of Joshua, huddling before a campfire twice as large as the one he built for himself. Each boy's face housed widened eyes shimmering with pure terror.

"You never see it coming for you in time." Brody tried to make his voice sound creepier while facing them from the other side of the fire pit. "A scratch from razor sharp tree claws across your shoulder is your only warning."

A tenderfoot near Joshua gasped. He glanced at his fellow

scout sharing the fallen log and saw trembling hands clutching both knees.

"One scratch." Brody raised his index finger. "If you feel it, do not turn around and look. No one lays eyes on the Scratcher and lives to tell the tale."

Once he issued this warning, the senior patrol leader naturally paused to let an uncomfortable silence settle over the rest of the troop. No younger scouts dared say a word or even breathe too loudly.

Twigs then snapped. One after another.

A tenderfoot down from Joshua let out a blood-curdling scream and jumped up from the log.

"Something scratched my shoulder!" he shrieked. "It's after me!"

At this point, Brody and other older scouts greeted his panic with unrestrained laughter. One of them emerged from the shadows behind the terrified tenderfoot, holding a branch with a sharpened end.

"Don't be so gullible bro," Brody said. "The scratcher isn't real."

The scratcher isn't real.

Joshua silently repeated those words after his mind circled back from that past campfire to the present one. The scratcher was an urban legend. Only a folktale tailor-made for pranking naive boy scouts. It belonged in the same category as a snipe hunt.

So why did this silent fear grip him, insisting those not-so-distant coyote howls acted as an omen foretelling a greater threat?

His ankle throbbed as Joshua scrambled off the slightly round boulder overlooking his fire pit and began setting up his tent.

He hunched over, methodically hammering each stake into the ground while trying to stay within hobbling distance of the pit. Joshua silently chided himself for not setting the tent up before he lost daylight. If wild animals were roaming nearby, he needed protection the tent would provide.

A growling scream rose above the crackling flames.

Joshua stiffened, tent stake in hand. He drew a sudden, sharp breath and straightened his back. Did his campfire attract a mountain lion?

Oh God. Of course, a predator would be lurking around here, scrounging for a midnight snack.

The scream repeated.

His eyes widened. Something seemed off with the second scream. Less like a mountain lion. It possessed an intense, guttural quality.

Like it came from …

Joshua's fingers tightened around the stake he had been ready to plant. He scrambled to his feet and doused the fire pit's dwindling flames with water and dirt. Did whatever lurked in the woods spot his campsite? He clenched his teeth as new pain burst through his sprained ankle. Joshua grabbed his backpack, still loaded with much of his gear, and shoved it through the open flap. He crawled in behind the backpack and zipped the flap up.

Maybe I acted fast enough to not draw attention.

Joshua clung to that hopeful thought like a buoy amid turbulent waves. His heart raced and he bit down on his lower lip again. No further calls sounded for several minutes. After his breathing slowed, Joshua relaxed his grip on the tent stake and let it fall to his side. He fished a flashlight out from a side pocket on his backpack.

Leaves crunched outside the tent.

Joshua's throat tightened. He was not alone.

Closing his eyes, he uttered a silent prayer. Joshua opened them again and crawled on his belly toward the tent flap. He nudged the zipper open a crack, pulling it in snail-like increments to maintain silence. Without a fire burning inside the pit, darkness reigned outside the tent. No more than outlines of surrounding trees were visible as his eyes slowly adjusted to the shadowy expanse.

A bipedal figure prowled around the pit. Joshua gnawed on his lower lip. Animals walked on all fours. A stranger must have wandered into his campsite. His heart refused to slow down. Did he stumble across a random psychopath who decided to stalk an injured solo camper? Joshua had seen far too many YouTube videos detailing similar scenarios to reject it out of hand.

His chest tightened. A cough tried to force itself out of his lungs. Joshua pushed back, trying to hold it in. His lungs burned and his throat shrank. Finally, a strained cough escaped past his lips.

The stranger stiffened. They wheeled around to face the tent.

Two glowing eyes met Joshua's gaze.

A chill raced through him from head to toe. Those eyes were neither fully human nor fully animal. One word clawed into his head and refused to leave.

Scratcher.

No. Joshua stayed motionless and pinched his eyelids shut. *The scratcher isn't real,* he insisted silently. *It's only a goofy campfire tale.*

Loud sniffs greeted his ears, mirroring a buck deer's snort. Joshua swallowed hard and cracked his eyes open again. A shadowy face pressed up against the tent flap.

Glowing eyes peeked through the opened zipper.

His lips trembled and tears trickled down both cheeks while Joshua fought an overpowering urge to scream. He dared not make the slightest movement or sound. Perhaps, the owner of those eyes did not see him or catch his scent. Maybe the creature would wander if he kept still. Joshua uttered a silent prayer again, pleading for this creature – whatever it was – to lose interest and leave him alone.

Low rumbling growls filled the tent.

Rough oak-like hands topped with wooden claws pulled the tent flap wider as the creature pushed through.

Joshua's fingers inched toward the tent stake at his side and wrapped around the tool's end. Fighting tremors, he clutched the stake and brought it forward. He slid backward a few inches while lying on his belly.

Claws sliced through the air, intending to tear into his face. Joshua thrust the stake forward and punctured the creature's forelimb. It let out a screeching yowl and ripped the injured limb out of his tent. Crunching leaves followed and grew increasingly fainter.

Joshua sat upright after silence returned and lingered long enough for him to feel satisfied the creature would not return. His hand still clutched the bloodied stake. Not even the cold numbness of his tight grip could induce him to relax that hand, even as his eyelids grew heavier, and sleep finally overtook him.

* * *

Once sunlight splashed over his eyelids again, Joshua didn't waste a second packing up his tent and his gear. Driving the creature off once amounted to a miracle. Staying here invited a second encounter and Joshua doubted his luck would carry over to a second night.

After twenty yards, intense pain burst through his injured ankle. An anguished groan escaped Joshua's lips. He limped over to the nearest boulder and dropped his pack off his shoulders.

"God. That ankle's worse than I thought," he mumbled, sitting atop the boulder.

Joshua grimaced and lifted his foot up onto an adjacent rock to elevate the purple ankle. Fishing out a map from a side pocket on his backpack, he studied it while trying to find his bearings. Going back down the mountain along the main trail would take longer than a day in his current condition.

"I can't stay here," Joshua said, casting a glance back at the clearing where he camped overnight. "Not with that creature lurking around in the woods."

Joshua couldn't bring himself to refer to the scratcher by its actual name. He didn't want to believe it existed in the real world instead of colorful urban legends. Still, no other animal or human being fit what he saw last night.

A monster, neither fully animal nor fully human, had tried to enter his tent. He pressed his hand to his forehead more than once to convince himself he wasn't suffering from a hallucination brought on by a fever.

He studied the map. The trailhead in Silver Fork Canyon was at least six miles away from his campsite. Dragonfly Lake was only about a mile further ahead. Covering a mile on his injured ankle would be difficult and painful, but his odds of reaching the lake were much more realistic. Search parties would more easily find him if he were at the actual lake.

Joshua put away the map and slid down the boulder. Using his folding saw, he lopped a thick branch off a dead pine tree nearby. Then, with his camping knife, Joshua fashioned the branch into a sturdy crutch.

Stories Joshua heard about the scratcher consumed his thoughts as he whittled away bark and knots while shaping the makeshift crutch. People in Deer Falls spread the stories around town long before Joshua was born. Their disparate tales agreed on a common nightmarish origin. What became the scratcher started life as a human being in the loosest sense.

Connor Hedges, a notorious serial killer, was said to have brought forth the scratcher. Hedges butchered 23 people during a decade-long spree across four states before fate turned against him. A routine traffic stop for speeding on a rural Utah highway led to Hedges' arrest and a death sentence for his horrific crimes.

While on death row, awaiting his execution, Hedges escaped from the Utah State Prison. He stole a pickup truck from a gas station in nearby Draper and fled across state lines to Colorado. Hedges evaded capture until an off-duty deputy sheriff spotted him at a bar only a mile outside of Deer Falls. The deputy recognized Hedges from his mug shot and tried to arrest him, but he fled through a backroom and raced up Silver Fork Canyon in his stolen truck.

Multiple deputies chased him up the winding canyon road and finally cornered the escaped serial killer at an isolated trailhead. Numerous bullets struck Hedges while he exchanged gunfire with deputies. He mustered enough strength to flee deeper into the woods surrounding the trail. The deputies pursued him, but he vanished in the forest. His blood trail ended at a fallen oak tree a mile from the stolen truck.

For an entire week, search teams on the ground and in the air combed the forest in every direction from the spot where Hedges' trail ran cold. Their search area spanned ten square miles. When no trace of Hedges turned up after seven days, the county sheriff declared him dead and called off the search.

Joshua never explored the trail where Hedges disappeared years earlier. His friends refused to hike in that part of the forest, insisting it became cursed ground because of what deputies found during their search.

Partial remains of two animal carcasses were found near the decaying tree where Hedges' blood trail ended. One belonged to a mountain lion. The other was a coyote. People claimed Hedges dabbled in black magic and used these wild animals and the tree to extend his life in an unnatural way.

People started disappearing soon after the search for Hedges ended. Hunters. Hikers. Snowmobilers. Weekend tourists who traversed the same section of the forest where he had vanished and met a similar fate.

Their stories flooded Joshua's mind. A dam built through pushing them aside had burst. Nothing held back these tales any longer. They consumed his full attention, leaving a stain of terror in their wake.

Every tale about the scratcher was relayed through the friend of a friend. Each fortunate survivor escaped from the deep woods where the monster allegedly dwelt. None claimed to have laid eyes on the scratcher itself. They only heard the scratcher's call. It sounded like a coyote at first, then a mountain lion as the monster drew closer. Only those lucky souls who heeded the warning call and fled – or found a way to avoid being detected – emerged from the forest unscathed.

The calls others reported hearing echoed what greeted Joshua last night. It was too much of a coincidence. What attacked him had to be the scratcher. No wild animal he knew fit what he saw and heard.

Forcing his body to bear him to the lake took on added importance. Not only did he want to make himself more visible to search parties, but camping along the lake's shoreline also offered a natural defense. Joshua would be able to see the scratcher emerging from the forest if it stalked him and attacked again after sundown.

He rose to his feet and tested out the finished crutch. It felt sturdy under his armpit. The crutch would hopefully shift enough weight off his ankle for Joshua to reach Dragonfly Lake early enough to set up camp and prepare traps to snare the creature.

* * *

Distorted shadows swallowed every tree surrounding Drag-onfly Lake after the last traces of sunlight vanished behind distant jagged peaks. Joshua kept a silent vigil near a newly constructed fire pit. Yellow flames crackled inside the rough rock circle. Dull aches spread from his muscles down to his bones on his arms and legs.

Once Joshua reached Dragonfly Lake, he spent the entire af-ternoon constructing traps. No obvious evidence the scratcher had tracked him showed up along the trail or around the lake. Still, Joshua wasn't naïve enough to assume he was now safe after winning a brief skirmish. The scratcher didn't strike him as a creature who would simply choose to ignore him and move onto other prey.

For his traps, he gathered a bundle of sticks. Joshua whittled one end of each stick into a sharp point and dug out a hole through the other end. Each hole was large enough to thread a nylon rope through the opening. He fished nylon rope out of his backpack and cut it into equal lengths before threading sections through multiple crude stakes. Joshua hung stakes from low-hanging branches at each trail leading to the portion of the lake where he set up camp. Then, he formed a trip wire between trees over each trail with the remaining rope.

Would the traps be enough?

Joshua wanted to believe he'd outsmart the scratcher. Camping by the lake offered a natural defense. He didn't think the monster could swim toward him without drawing unwanted attention and he also hoped his traps would at least slow the scratcher down long enough for him to run and hide.

Darkening shadows limited visibility beyond the fire pit. Given enough time, Joshua would have set mounted torches between his new campsite and the forest. Abundant flames may not have deterred the creature's return. It showed no qualms about approaching his fire pit a night earlier.

With his back to the lake, Joshua stared out into shadowy trees clustering the slope before him. His eyes trailed from trap to trap. He set three traps in between mandatory rests for his ankle. His walking stick now lay at his side, ready to be snatched off the ground at a moment's notice.

An intense howl pierced the silence.

Joshua stiffened. Breaths left his mouth in quick shallow bursts. A chill crawled down his spine like a silent tarantula.

Other howls joined the first, mimicking the cadence from the previous night. Joshua licked his lips and swallowed hard. His heart raced faster.

The scratcher is here. Oh God. The scratcher is here.

Howls soon gave way to angry growling screams. Joshua's hand dropped to his belt line and unbuttoned the sheath on his camping knife. If he was fast enough, the sturdy six-inch steel blade would fend off any sudden attack.

Silence settled over his campsite with an unexpected suddenness. No howls. No growls. Not even chirping from random crickets. The earlier calls shined a light on the monster's direction and distance from him. This silence felt even more terrifying than the scratcher's calls.

Where did it go?

Joshua stared past violent flickers within the fire pit. His fingers circled the handle of his knife, clenching it tight. He felt like cornered prey frantically trying to avoid becoming a predator's late-night snack. No doubt the scratcher had stalked him, since before sunset, waiting for a perfect moment to strike.

A bipedal figure cut through his peripheral vision. Swift and fleeting with the speed of a shadow or phantom. Joshua searched for signs or sounds indicating the scratcher sprang a trap and sent stakes raining down from above. Nothing he wanted to hear pierced the agonizing silence.

Claws dug into Joshua's shoulder, tearing through fabric and flesh with ease. He screamed. An arm wrenched him backward and he tumbled to the ground near the fire pit.

The scratcher stood over Joshua. A low rumbling growl escaped its lips. Flames cast a dull glow upon the creature, revealing a body and face perfectly blending mountain lion, coyote, and human features. All cooked together into a terrifying feral stew. Coarse yellow-brown fur covered a sleek, muscular frame. Razor-sharp claws tipped each finger. Both hands seemed to be carved from tree branches, shaped to mimic human hands covered in bark.

Blood dripped from the scratcher's claws.

Joshua winced and traced his fingers over the sheath. The knife hadn't fallen out.

Thank God.

"I'm not afraid of you."

Dark fierce eyes settled on Joshua, offering a glimpse of the scratcher's savage soulless nature. No traces of humanity were left. Only an animalistic drive to kill and destroy.

"I refuse to be afraid of you."

A tremor creeping into his voice betrayed Joshua's attempted bravado. Dismay seized him over knowing this monster silently dodged his traps to reach the fire pit untouched. Panic gripped every bone and muscle in his body. Joshua wanted to sprint to the shore and dive in the lake, hoping to conceal himself amid shadowy water until the scratcher departed.

Running away wasn't in the hand fate dealt him. Even with two healthy ankles, Joshua still lacked enough foot speed to outrun this creature. Trying to hobble away on one good leg only invited a quick and brutal death.

Facing the monster was his only option.

Joshua unsheathed his knife. The scratcher's ears flattened against its skull. It bared jagged yellowing teeth and unleashed a growling hiss.

"I won't hide this time," Joshua said.

The scratcher started circling him and then lunged forward in one sudden fluid motion. Joshua veered away from swiping claws and thrust out his knife blade. It sliced across the creature's left palm, peeling back bark. His attacker recoiled with a pained growl, pulled back, and glanced down at its wounded hand, much like a human would do.

"Hedges?"

That single word drew a flicker of recognition from the monster's eyes. The scratcher stared at him menacingly as if their encounter had suddenly grown much more personal than hunting an evening meal.

Simply wounding this creature wasn't good enough now. Joshua couldn't let it flee back into the forest. Survival meant slaying the scratcher. If Joshua failed, how many more innocent people would lose their lives to this unholy monster? Ending the serial killer's life would shut a door that should already have permanently sealed long ago.

Keeping his knife in front of him, Joshua scrambled to his feet and backed his heels up against stones forming part of the fire pit. Heat from the flames soaked into his calves. The scratcher lunged at him again. It swiped at his knife with the uninjured forelimb but missed.

Joshua's wounded shoulder and ankle throbbed from pain. He clenched his teeth and drew a sharp breath but held his ground.

"One of us will be dead before the night is over," Joshua said, eyes squarely fixed on the creature. "I plan on it being you."

The scratcher snarled and charged forward, barreling straight into him like an angry bull. Both fell into the diminutive fire. Burning sticks scattered inside the pit and hot embers shot skyward. Joshua's knife flew out of his hand. He let out a pained shout as flames pressed against exposed flesh.

A piercing yowl drowned out his own scream. Seared hair and skin meshed into a pungent aroma. Joshua pushed the scratcher away from him and crawled out of the fire pit. He rolled over to snuff out the nascent flames in his burning clothes.

Smoke wafted up from the creature's right side as the scratcher rose to its feet. It attacked a third time. Tree claws sank into Joshua's right hip. He screamed again. The pursuing scratcher tugged on his leg and dragged him backward.

Floating embers from the scattered fire revealed the camping knife. It lay in the dirt a few feet away. If Joshua could only reach the handle, he'd end this.

He had to end this before the creature tore him to shreds.

Joshua twisted his leg and kicked wildly at the scratcher. His injured foot struck the creature's forearm, causing it to stumble. He wrenched his leg free of the scratcher's grasp and scrambled toward the knife. When his fingers clenched the handle again, Joshua rolled onto his back and brought the blade forward.

The scratcher quickly regained its balance and charged Joshua a second time. Clumps of hair were missing where flames had burned flesh. Severe burns pockmarked the right side of the monster's torso.

Joshua thrust the knife upward as the scratcher closed the scant distance between them. His blade plunged between the creature's ribs. A growing scream escaped the monster's lips while it simultaneously raked claws across his chest. Blood dribbled from its open mouth, and it staggered. He withdrew the blade and struck again and again.

After the third blow, the scratcher lurched forward and fell to the ground. Eyes glassed over as it let out a gurgling groan.

Joshua lay on the ground, panting, waiting to see if the scratcher moved again. Once he was satisfied it no longer drew breath, he tried to stand but stumbled and fell to his knees. Blood dripped from his chest wound into dry forest soil.

He coughed as lingering smoke passed by his face and rose to his feet. Joshua stumbled over to his tent and drew a first aid kit out of his backpack. Pulling out a roll of gauze and antiseptic ointments, he bound deep scratches across his chest and treated burns covering his left side. At best, a temporary solution until a search and rescue party showed up. His eyelids grew heavy after tending to the injuries he could reach.

Joshua awoke after dawn to a distant helicopter humming. His whole body felt sore and weak from blood loss. After crawling out of the tent, he limped to the nearby shore. The scratcher's lifeless body lay unmoved from the spot where it fell only a few hours earlier. Joshua waved his uninjured arm frantically and called out to the approaching helicopter, hoping the pilot would see him.

John Coon is an accomplished author and journalist. As a journalist, he has written for the Associated Press, the Washington Post, the Boston Globe, the Los Angeles Times, and many other distinguished publications worldwide. John has covered many major sporting events including March Madness and the NBA Playoffs. As an author, he has published several popular novels including the Alien People Chronicles trilogy. Subscribe to his author newsletter, Strange New Worlds, at newworlds.substack.com. John is a graduate of the University of Utah and currently resides in Utah.

III

The Thorny One of the Water

By: Mike Sullivan

The Thorny One of the Water

With a high-pitched screech of brakes, and a severe dip of the front end, the rusty, old Ford Bronco came to an abrupt stop and Patrick Byrnes breathed a sigh of relief. He'd been on planes flying through extreme turbulence that had bumped and jostled less. His teeth ached from where they'd clacked together several times, and a headache spread backward from his forehead. Patrick envied Rafa, the old man sitting next to him. He wore those giant side-shield sunglasses, an LA Dodgers baseball cap, and seemed completely unfazed by the rugged ride. Glancing down, Patrick saw why. Rafa had wedged a small pillow between his butt and the thin, vinyl backseat cushion. Obviously, this was not his first rodeo with this bucking Bronco.

Stepping down from the old SUV, Patrick coughed and waved away the billow of dust and exhaust flowing forward. He looked back at the dirt road they had just traversed. The word *road* gave it too much credit. It was more a wide, glorified path that years of travel had grooved through the jungle. There was a massive divot, pit, or cleft every couple of feet and the Bronco's driver, Matias, avoided none of them. Not surprising since Matias was a gangly fourteen-year-old boy with scabby knees.

Matias was the youngest son of Miguel, the Bronco's fourth passenger, and Patrick's Mexican guide. Patrick had contacted several guides before he found one available at such short notice and willing to comply with Patrick's definitive, non-negotiable requests, the most important being that Patrick would trek alone into the forest. Miguel had argued against that stipulation at first, but he eventually agreed to the terms. When Miguel arrived at the hostel outside Mexico City that morning, Matias and Rafa, who was Miguel's father-in-law, were in the Bronco with him. Patrick hadn't said anything when the boy, after loading Patrick's gear into the rear cargo space, swapped places with Miguel and climbed into the driver's seat. Patrick figured, *When in Rome. Or in Mexico ...* Now his throbbing tailbone made him wish he had spoken up.

Matias jumped down from the driver's seat with a big grin, darted to the rear, and popped open the cargo door. He reminded Patrick of his son, Peter. Pete had also smiled big. Patrick stretched his back and reached into his pocket for a tip for the boy. Not yet noon and the heat was already borderline oppressive. *Great day for a hike,* he thought as he removed his wide-brimmed hat, wiping sweat from his forehead with his forearm. He looked to his left. The dense, green jungle. An intimidating, thick terrain of trees, branches, and vines. His destination was several miles ahead, straight through those trees.

Patrick heard another door open and close, then dry dirt crunching under boots as Miguel ambled over. His guide wore ironed blue jeans — a crease sharp enough to slice bread traversed the legs — and a short-sleeved khaki shirt.

"Second thoughts?" Miguel asked. He removed a small comb from his shirt pocket and drew it through his impressive walrus mustache.

"Nope."

"The boy's a good driver, no? Ready for American highways?"

Patrick chuckled.

"Good driver? Sure. But your vehicle needs some work, I think. The brakes sound like a shrieking tea kettle. And your shocks…"

Miguel smiled and put his comb away.

"What shocks?"

They both laughed.

"Right," Patrick said.

"*Señor*, I'm sorry to keep asking, but I feel I must. You are sure about this? Very sure?"

Patrick looked around him and then his eyes settled on Miguel again.

"Yep," he said. "I'm sure."

"It's not too late to get you into a tour group. Take the safer trail …"

Patrick rubbed his face. The three-day beard was rough, itchy. He knew he looked run down. He was too thin (*practically skin and bones*, his mother would say) and in contrast to Miguel, everything Patrick wore was wrinkled and ill-fitting. He glanced up at the cloudless sky and wondered what shade of blue he was seeing. When his son had been a toddler, he liked to go through his crayon box and ask Patrick to read the different names. Peter loved blue, and he was amazed there could be so many different hues. His favorite was called "bluetiful" by Crayola and that was the color of the sky today — bluetiful.

"I'm aware, Miguel. You've mentioned it a few times." Patrick looked at the guide again. "You're still getting your full fee."

"Yes, forgive me. It's not the fee. Going in there *sólo*." He pointed to the jungle. "That is what bothers me."

"It's just a few miles, right? You said yourself. One night. I've done it before."

"But not in Mexico."

"True."

"Maybe, if you'd tell me why you insist on going into the jungle alone? Maybe I'd understand."

A grunt came from behind them, and both men turned towards the sound.

"It's heavy." Patrick said to Matias. The boy had practically doubled over from the weight of Patrick's backpack. Dust flew up as he plopped the pack down at Patrick's feet. Patrick handed the boy a few bucks. Matias glanced over at his father, who gave him a paternal nod of approval.

"*¡Muchas gracias!*"

Matias gleefully took the offered bills and shoved the money into his pocket.

Patrick slid his eyes from Matias to Miguel. Father and son bore a striking resemblance to one another. They were almost the same height, but Matias was still in that awkward teen growth phase where his arms and legs were all out of proportion to his torso. He had his father's nose — slightly crooked — and the same thin mouth and pointed chin. They both had a full head of thick hair. Matias's was shaggy and jet black. His father's was combed perfectly, more salt than pepper.

"You really want to know why?" Patrick asked, directing his question to Miguel.

"It would make it easier for me to sleep tonight, *Señor*. I have guided many to the ruins. Groups of three, four, five, ten, more. But you are the first to pay for a guide and yet you refuse to be guided. It is not a risky trip, when you take the right trails, but … *la jungla*, the jungle … She can be unpredictable."

Patrick understood Miguel's worries. If something happened out there, if he got lost, or hurt, Miguel could get into trouble. Guides were supposed to guide, after all. Not let their customer wander off alone into a dense jungle. But Patrick wasn't a complete novice. As a younger man, he had camped and hiked all over the U.S. The Appalachian Trail, the Long Trail in Vermont, the Continental Divide, plus many off-the-beaten-path adventures. It had been more than twenty years since he had hiked and slept outdoors, but he was ready.

"The short answer is, I made a promise."

Squatting down, Patrick opened his pack, started removing items, and placed them on the ground. The impromptu trip from Boston to this remote part of Mexico had been both long and taxing. He'd checked his gear at home and back at the hotel, but he wanted Miguel to see that he had come prepared. It didn't take him long to have all his stuff laid out on the ground: tent and sleeping bag, rain jacket, first-aid kit, enough food for two days, three three-liter soft water bottles and a gravity filtration device (according to Miguel, his camping site would be next to a small river), waterproof matches, a serrated knife, a small shovel, battery-powered lantern, and a 1000 lumen LED flashlight.

Going over his equipment gave him an excuse not to answer Miguels' question, but he felt the man's eyes fixed on him waiting for a deeper explanation. He instead glanced over at the guide's son.

"Hey Matias. How old are you?" Patrick reached deep into his limited Spanish. "Uh, *¿cuantos … anos … tienes?*"

"*Catorce.* Four-teens."

Patrick nodded.

"Fourteen. Good age."

He picked up the small lantern. Turned it on and off a couple of times.

"I had a son. His name was Peter." Patrick pulled one other item from the backpack — a red and blue child's plastic lunchbox covered with pictures of Spider-Man. Two strips of silver duct tape aided a small clasp in keeping it closed. He had been worried about bringing it on the plane and through customs. But he had brought more paperwork than he needed, including Peter's passport, and there were no issues. "This was his."

Matias' eyes lit up.

"With great power …"

"Comes great responsibility." Patrick finished the famous refrain. "You like Spidey?"

Matias nodded. Miguel ruffled his son's hair.

"The boy's always reading the *historietas*," he said.

"Comic books?"

Miguel nodded.

"Yeah. Peter loved comic books, too." Patrick looked at the lunch box in his hands. "Spider-Man was his favorite. He liked the colors of his suit."

"What happened to your son?" Miguel asked.

Patrick didn't answer right away. He looked at the sky again and changed his mind about the shade. He decided today's sky was more indigo. Finally, he blew out a breath.

"He died."

"*Te acompaño en el sentimiento,*" Miguel said with respect.

Patrick assumed Miguel was offering his condolences.

"*Gracias,*" he said. "Yeah, he was sick for a long time. In the hospital. We, his mother and I, wearen't together anymore, but we would sit in the room with him every day. Watch TV. Talk."

As he spoke, Patrick started re-packing his gear. He checked to make sure the lunch box was closed securely and then put it back in first, shoving it down to the bottom, followed by the compact tent. "One day, and this was near the end, Pete, he was so tiny. Weighed as much as a piece of paper. We were watching TV. Some documentary on Nat Geo or something. I don't remember exactly."

Next went in the small lantern and the flashlight. Then the jacket. "For some reason, Pete had really gotten into these travel shows. So, we were all watching this show. It was about your ruins here." With the knife, Patrick gestured out towards the trees. Then he put it into the side pockets of the backpack. "After the show ended Pete looked at me. I hadn't seen him so excited in months. He turned to me and said, 'Dad! Look at those trees. So green! When I get better, let's go there. Will you take me?'"

Patrick stopped repacking for a moment. He stared off into the jungle, but his eyes saw his son in the cramped hospital room at Boston Children's Hospital instead of a legion of trees. Attached by rubber tubes and wires to all sorts of glowing beeping machines. Dying.

"I told him, 'Absolutely. I promise.' Then he laid down, suddenly tired. It took so much energy for him just to be happy. 'Awesome,' he said. He fell asleep smiling."

Patrick smiled at the memory himself. A sad smile. He hated telling this story. It brought back all the emotions. Crushing guilt. Powerful anger. Talking about Peter to another dad —who still had his son — made it worse. He yanked the pack's straps tight and shoved the sleeping bag on top. "He never woke up. Died the next day. He was ten years old." Patrick pulled extra hard on the straps around the rolled sleeping bag, checked all the other clasps and catches on the backpack. He checked them twice. He did not want to look back at Miguel and Matias. It hurt.

"A sad story." Miguel turned away from Patrick. "*Es triste aunque es ley de vida, la muerte llega cuando menos la esperamos...*" he said in a low voice.

"I didn't get all of that, Miguel," Patrick stood and turned to face the guide. "But I got the end. Death does indeed come when we least expect it. That's the goddamned sucker punch, isn't it?"

He swung the backpack on and distributed the weight across his shoulders and back. Patrick buckled the front support belt.

"I made a promise to my dying son. It's something I need to do alone. Can't be around a bunch of tourists."

An awkward silence followed, broken only by sounds of the Mexican jungle. Bird calls and caws, cicadas, wind. A loud crack of a branch — perhaps broken by an animal or simply a dead tree and gravity. Inhaling through his nose, Patrick took note of the jungle's unique smell for the first time. Vegetation and flora. Mud and rot. Neither pleasant nor sour. Both. Natural. Nothing manmade.

Miguel frowned at Matias, turned back to Patrick, and nodded.

"I understand, *Señor.*" He walked over to the Bronco and brought out a machete with a belt and sheath and handed them to Patrick. "You'll want this. The trail is not used often, so there will be growth. This way. I'll show you where to begin."

Patrick adjusted the pack one final time and followed the guide. They walked along the road, past where Matias had stopped the Bronco. As he passed the rear passenger door, Rafa reached out and grabbed Patrick's arm. The Old Man began speaking to him in rapid Spanish. Much too fast for Patrick to follow. He caught a few words–*perro de agua, no Seguro*—but wasn't completely confident of their meaning. With a surprisingly strong grip, Rafa clamped onto Patrick's wrist, and with his other hand, started violently pointing and gesturing to the jungle beyond. At one point, the old man held up a leathery, gnarled hand, his fingers bent into a twisted claw, and swiped it through the air in front of Patrick's face.

Matias climbed back into the cab, frowning at his grandfather.

"What's he saying?" Patrick asked the boy.

Matias didn't answer.

Miguel made his way over. "He wants you to be careful. Stay on the path. Don't wander into the jungle. Many critters in there." Then, turning to Rafa, he said, *"¡Papá! ¡Deja de tonterías! ¡No existe el perro de agua!"*

Patrick smiled at the old man.

"Gracias. I'll be careful."

"He doesn't speak English," Matias said.

Patrick tried to find Rafa's eyes through the lenses of the old man's huge sunglasses. He only saw his own distorted reflection. He gently extricated his arm, tapped Rafa's hand, and said *"Gracias,"* again.

Miguel showed Patrick where the trail began, and then the guide got in the Bronco and Matias started the old engine. Patrick waved as they passed and, even with the massive sunglasses covering his eyes, he knew Rafa still stared at him as they drove away.

Patrick wondered about the things Rafa had said. He didn't

think Miguel gave him an exact translation. Patrick felt like the old man imparted a warning of some kind. A warning about a danger in the jungle. But wouldn't Miguel have told him if there was something dangerous among the trees? Above him, clouds lidded the sun. Rafa's Spanish floated about in his head as he entered the shadowed jungle.

Something about dogs, he thought. *Dogs in the water?*

* * *

Patrick was exhausted. Even absent, Miguel was a good guide. His directions had been spot-on. The sinuous trail between the trees had indeed become overgrown with lower vegetation, but Patrick got through it with the machete and patience. Miguel told him this trail used to be the only path leading to the ruins. Growing publicity and interest convinced the Mexican government to clear out a larger section of jungle to allow bigger tour groups to approach the ruins from the front. Since then, this trail became less traveled. Based on all the overgrowth along the path, Patrick guessed he was the first one in many years to travel along this trail.

Reaching the river took him most of the day. He found a perfect area, matching what Miguel described earlier, to set up the tent just a few yards from the water. He refilled his bottles with filtered water and ate some granola and dried fruit. Tomorrow, he planned to follow the river directly and approach the ruins from the rear by midday.

Patrick let himself sit and relax for the first time in many days. It had been a long journey in a short amount of time. *When did the journey start, really?* he wondered. Had it started five days ago when he boarded the plane at Logan? Or did it start three months ago when Peter died? Or a year before that when Peter was first diagnosed? Had his whole life been leading to this moment in a jungle in Mexico?

Ugh, I'm turning into a fucking philosopher. Or a piss-poor songwriter.

The disease that killed Peter came from nowhere, attacking him like a monster from the dark. It seemed as if one minute he listened to Peter cry and coo in his crib and the next he sat at his bedside in the hospital. In truth, he had seven healthy years with Peter. His son was like any other boy. He liked to run. He liked riddles. He liked Bugs Bunny cartoons, ice cream, and cinnamon toast. He put ketchup on everything. He could be moody and stubborn, but he was never mean.

Those years went by so fucking fast. Patrick wished he could have every extra minute he had stayed late at work back again and use that time to spend with his son. He always thought there would be more time. Tomorrow. Next weekend. But there wasn't. Cancer came from the dark and stole it all away.

They say there are five stages of grief. Or is it six? Doesn't matter. As far as Patrick was concerned there was one — anger. It made no sense that a child — innocent, pure, should get sick with something as cruel as cancer. When a person has aged and the machine has been running full time for years, it makes sense it would wind down. Parts would get worn, be susceptible to damage. But a child? Fresh off the lot? All the pieces are brand new. They should work perfectly. For Patrick, it just didn't make any sense. The pure random nature and unfairness of disease made him so angry. He'd been angry every day for over a year. It grew inside him, fed off him, just like the tumor that had grown inside Peter. Hopefully, after this trip to the ruins, he would be able to stop being angry and begin to heal.

Hopefully.

Patrick pulled the Spider-Man lunchbox from his backpack and put it on the ground beside him. His thoughts returned to Peter and his crayons. What would he have thought about these greens? Much different from the New England forests. During the spring and summer back home, browns and grays were in greater abundance in the deep woods. The green seemed to retreat upwards into the treetops. Here in Mexico, the greens grew stronger while traveling into the jungle's depths. Emerald hues covered the ground and lower plant life.

Now, the setting sun's orange rays broke through the tree canopy like blades of giant, golden swords, giving everything a fiery glow. It stirred another memory for Patrick. He had woken up in the uncomfortable chair in Peter's hospital room. Sleep was as infrequent then as now and Patrick often found himself drifting at odd times. Peter was sitting straight up in his bed, looking over Patrick's shoulder at the slim west-facing window. The view was uneventful. Just ordinary buildings surrounding that section of Boston Children's Hospital.

"What're you looking at, Pete?" Patrick asked.

Peter didn't answer right away, letting silence linger for a moment.

"Just watching the sun go down," he finally said

Patrick turned to look. He'd been in this room, this chair, for so many days and not once thought of watching the sunset. He spied a little bit of glowing yellows and oranges through the structures and reflecting off glass windows as the sun dipped below the concrete horizon.

"I know it's not the best view," Peter said. "But every sunset is pretty. It's nice to see them. Don't you think?"

Patrick turned back and glanced at his son.

"Sure Pete. You're absolutely right."

Patrick shook his head, trying to shake away the memory while watching the resplendent sunset before him.

"Ah, Pete," he said out loud. "If only you could see this one."

And soon, like every other night for the past three months, Patrick fell asleep wishing to see his son again.

* * *

"Dad!"

Patrick awoke with a start. Did he hear Peter calling out to him? The jungle was painted with darkness. Patrick sat up, rubbed his eyes. Something was odd. He blinked a few times. He could see too much for the middle of the night. Deep in the jungle, darkness surrounding him, and yet Patrick saw his surroundings perfectly. He imagined this was how night time predators saw the world.

"Dad."

Peter's voice again. Patrick didn't know if he heard a real voice or if he was experiencing a particularly vivid memory or a dream. Whatever was happening, it seemed quite real. He stood up slowly, turning, trying to follow the sound.

Peter's hospital bed stood before him in the middle of the jungle. Blue-white moonlight stabbed straight down through the trees, spotlighting Peter as if he were a performer on center stage. Tiny motes danced inside shafts of moonlight. Peter sat ramrod straight in the bed, looking directly at Patrick. The bed was surrounded by the same assortment of beeping machines that had been in his hospital room. All the things that had hung from the ceiling in the hospital, various tubes and wires, now hung from the trees like vines, twisting around bed rails.

Patrick slowly walked closer. Peter's lips moved, but no sound came from his mouth. That's when Patrick realized there was no sound at all. Nothing. As if someone had hit *mute* on the jungle remote control.

As he drew closer to Peter's bed, he finally heard a sound fading in from the river behind him. It sounded human. A wail or a sob. Patrick stopped and turned and listened more closely.

What is that?

The sobbing stopped as quickly as it started and eerie silence returned. When he turned back, Peter and the hospital bed had disappeared and were replaced by something equally incongruous. A baby's crib. Peter's crib. The same crib Patrick had assembled himself two months before Peter came into the world. The crib he and Peter's mother had wheeled into their tiny bedroom after bringing Peter home from the hospital because they couldn't bear to be separated from him. Not even by the thin walls of their tiny apartment.

He took a step toward the crib. Just one step. He didn't want to go any closer and see what lay in the crib. Whatever it was, he knew it would be something bad.

Patrick heard the sound again.

A baby crying.

Patrick awoke with a start again; the baby's cry was still fresh in his ears. *What was that?* He was groggy, still half-asleep and wondering if he was truly awake this time. *A baby?* His thoughts were jumbled, unclear. *No.* The sound came from his dream, that's all. Just a little stone tossed over the wall by his subconscious. Happens all the time, right? Still, something seemed wrong. He shook his head. Rubbed and lightly slapped his face, waking himself up more fully. He dreamed about Peter almost every night. There were good ones and bad ones. But this one was unlike any before.

Patrick unzipped his sleeping bag and crawled out of his tent. Unlike in the dream, he could see next to nothing. The darkness was Stygian, hiding almost everything within it. Moonlight struggled to get through the trees and the night had desaturated all color. The trees were black. The river, with no tree canopy to block it, was lit by a sickle-blade moon and a scattering of stars. Patrick heard water flowing, but not much else. A soft susurrus of tree leaves blowing in the wind, but no animal life. No insects chirping. No frogs croaking. The jungle sounds he heard before he fell asleep had stopped. Not the dead silence from his dream, but close.

It was creepy.

He took a step away from his camp. He still wore his boots, so he was unconcerned about stepping on anything in the dark. Could a baby be out here somewhere? That's ridiculous. Even if someone else was hiking in this area, they wouldn't bring along a baby. An infant? No way. He began to doubt he heard anything. The sound hadn't repeated.

It must have been in my head.

But he didn't return to his tent. Patrick was fully awake now. The sound of the dream and the way it subsumed his consciousness concerned him. He stood still. Trying to isolate and identify every snap, every rustle, every whisper.

There! Unmistakable.

He clearly heard a baby's cry somewhere nearby. Patrick couldn't ignore it. More and more horrible scenarios flew through his mind. Spiders. Scorpions. A hungry jaguar. God, a giant snake could be about to swallow the baby whole.

The human cries seemed to come from Patrick's left, closer to the river. He grabbed the machete and flashlight and slowly stepped that way, waiting for another cry to lead him. He flicked the flashlight on and swept the beam before him, left to right and up and down.

After just a few steps he heard the cry again. Yes, it came from near the water. His feet sank into soft mud as he crept up on the river's edge. Black muck and soft moss squished under his boots. A rotten-egg smell from the water pierced his nostrils. The current bubbled softly, like the small vaporizer they put in Peter's room when he was a baby. Not too far away he thought he saw a long, black snake slicing through the water. Patrick shuddered. He was not a fan of snakes in general, but ones that lived in the water really freaked him out.

The baby had stopped crying. What happened to it? Patrick looked left and right. He could only see a few feet up and down the river. The water splashed off to the side and he jumped, spun around. At his feet sat a grumpy lump of a bullfrog frowning up at him, its bumpy skin shiny in the moonlight. Patrick chuckled. *Get a grip, dude.* Another frog leapt from the water and dropped next to the first. *That's weird,* Patrick thought. The two froggy pals hopped away from the river into the jungle together.

Patrick's heart was beating fast. He felt very vulnerable. The fact of his alone-ness struck him hard. *This was a dumb idea. No one knows where I am.* Well, that wasn't entirely true. Miguel knew where he was and where he was going.

An emotion he hadn't felt since he was a child suddenly overcame him, and it took him a moment to even recognize the feeling.

Patrick was scared.

He turned on the flashlight. Its LED beam cleft the dark but didn't help Patrick's uneasiness.

Something was very wrong here. Off. Odd.

His brain screamed at him to run… just leave everything and beat feet.

But he didn't listen. He ignored what he considered a childish gut reaction and forced his inner adult to reassert control.

There is nothing out there. Stop thinking like a child.

He inhaled, held his breath for four beats, then blew it out.

But if there's nothing out there, then what is crying?

Patrick sensed hidden eyes following him. Someone, or some*thing*, watched him. He turned in a tight circle. His heart began to beat even faster. Sweat dripped from his brow, the salt stinging his eye. He tightened his grip on the machete and turned away from the river to face the forest. Within the sweeping flashlight beam, he saw his small camp and just a few gray trees. Pitch blackness beyond. Was someone out there in the blackness, waiting to strike? Thoughts about drug dealers and bandits flashed through Patrick's mind. Or maybe a hungry animal?

The baby cried out again. Patrick jerked and almost cried out himself. This time the sound was different. It went on longer, began to shift, sounding less human. It morphed into a low growl before it stopped.

Quiet.

The silence became almost more upsetting than the cries.

An unmistakable sodden sound of something emerging from the river behind him pierced the silence with sudden sharpness. A guttural, low snarl of an animal followed. He felt a tightness in his chest and the flashlight beam began to quiver.

Patrick turned just as a creature leapt upon him.

It collided with Patrick square in the chest, knocking him hard to the ground. Both machete and flashlight flew from his hands.

Patrick lay in the mud, unable to catch his breath. A beast no larger than a small dog, with wet black fur that stood up like thorns along its back, sat on his chest. It stared down at Patrick with red, beady eyes. Black lips pulled back from silver fangs and long strips of clear drool dripped onto his face.

Patrick couldn't move. Fear, shock, disorientation all kept him immobilized. What was this creature? What was happening?

Short, pointed ears laid back against the monster's head. The creature's long and thin tail slashed back and forth through the air like a bullwhip. This was no ordinary tail. It blended into a human hand at the tip, a hand equipped with sharp, barbed claws instead of fingernails on all five fingers.

"Jesus Christ!"

More rivulets of drool dripped from the creature's jaws. Warm spit hit Patrick's skin and slithered down his cheeks like worms into his open mouth. The thing's lips began to quiver.

It's gonna bite me!

With that thought, his paralysis ended. He shoved the creature. Rolled. The thing skidded through the mud and landed on its side.

Patrick scrambled to his feet. The thing raised itself up on all fours and bent forward, red eyes staring at Patrick.

It made that guttural growl again. Patrick felt, more than he heard, the sound. Deep in his belly. Then the growl shifted again. Changed. Became the cry of a human baby. A human infant's cry came from this savage monster's lips. And then it changed again. Back into an untamed animal growl. Patrick was shocked. This... this what? Animal? Creature? Monster?

Whatever faced him had mimicked the cry of a human being as *bait*. To *lure* him to the river.

Something moved in the corner of Patrick's vision. He arched back at the waist just as the thing's tail whipped past his face. Sharp claws on the bizarre hand at the tail's tip tore through the air.

Patrick glanced away from the creature, searching for the machete. It hadn't fallen far. He took two giant steps to the right, grabbed the weapon, and turned to face the creature. Just as Patrick raised the machete, the thing's tail snapped forward. The claws grabbed the machete by the dirty blade, tore it from his hand, and threw it into the river.

Patrick barely had a moment to register what had happened before the creature let out an inhuman screech and lunged again. He raised his arms to protect himself, but the creature hit him with enough force to knock Patrick off his feet. He fell backward, hitting his head on the ground. The blow to his head and the pure unbelievability of the situation left Patrick feeling stunned. He grabbed the thing's neck and pushed to keep its mouth—and teeth—away from his throat. But again, he forgot about the tail… until it sliced through the air with a big rock in its hand. The creature pummeled Patrick's already injured head with the rock.

It hit him hard.

It hit him again.

He was on the edge of unconsciousness. His vision was blurry and darkened. Thinking was clogged.

The water was a shock when the creature shoved his face into the shallows of the river and held his head under. Patrick began to flail his arms and legs. Water foamed and sprayed around him. The creature was powerful. Patrick couldn't shake it off his back. A hand on the back of his head pushed him down further into the water. He knew—just knew—it was the one on the tip of the tail. He struggled but wasn't strong enough to free himself. Under the water, thick rivulets of blood sunk in ribbons past his eyes. The tail shoved his head down even harder into the river silt at the bottom. Tiny pieces of dirt and stone scratched his cheeks. His eyes.

"Dad…"

He heard Peter again. Patrick opened his mouth and inhaled. Water filled his lungs.

* * *

Matias walked unafraid through the jungle. His granddad, *Abuelo* Rafa, told him stories about strange creatures that lived among the trees since he was a small boy, but they were just stories. No such thing as monsters. Besides, it was just about noon. If monsters were in the jungle, they would never come out in the bright sunshine.

He searched for the American. Three days had passed, and the American had not returned from his trip to the ruins. *Papá* was worried. He said he would have to go find the man. *Abuelo* Rafa said it was a waste of time. As they argued, Matias decided he would find the missing American. He would be a hero. Just like Spider-Man. The American had that *interesante* lunchbox with Spider-Man. Perhaps the American would give it to him as a reward. He was too old to use a lunchbox. The kids at school would laugh. But Matias thought anything with Spider-Man was cool.

The thought that something bad may have happened to the American never crossed Matias's mind. Not until he got to the destroyed campsite. There was stuff strewn everywhere. The tent was slashed to shreds. Same with the sleeping bag. It looked like monkeys had gone nuts, except the American's food was untouched. Matias found the bag of granola and stuff under what remained of the tent. Wild animals would have eaten the food. What else would have done this? People?

Matias suddenly grew fearful.

A cloud covered the sun and light left the jungle.

Matias saw something red and blue. The lunchbox. Open, broken into two pieces. Next to it a large, thick, plastic bag. It had also been slashed open. Harsh gray sand had spilled from the bag. It had spread onto the ground and been blown into the water.

Matias was about to head home when something in the river caught his eye. Something strange. Matias walked closer to the water. The gurgling sound of the current seemed extra loud to his ears. It wasn't clear what he was looking at until his feet were practically in the water. Once he realized what it was, he threw up his breakfast.

He'd found the American.

The body lay face up in the mud, half in and half out of the river. Water ran down between the legs, around his bare feet. His head faced the shore. Black and bloody pits were where eyes should have been. The man's mouth was wide open, his broken jaw hung low. It swayed and bobbed slowly as the river water flowed past as if the dead man were trying to speak. All his teeth were missing. His fingernails and toenails had been ripped out.

Matias knew what had happened here and drew no closer to the body. He backed away slowly, turned, and fled. Ran back home. *Abuelo* Rafa had told him stories about the creatures that lived in the jungle. In the rivers. And what they did to people drawn to the water by their awful mimicry. They ate the eyes, the teeth, the fingernails. He had to get home. Tell *Papá* and *Abuelo* Rafa. They had to make sure no one touched the dead man's body. Anyone who touches a victim will become a victim themselves. They needed *el sacerdote* — the priest. Only a holy man can touch someone attacked by these creatures from myth. *El perro de agua* — the Water Dog. The Thorny One of the Water. *El Ahuizotl.*

The sound of a baby crying behind him only made him run faster.

Mike Sullivan started writing short scripts for a film class and turned that love of film into a profession. After years of editing documentary films, reading works of others, and raising a family, Mike started writing stories. They were dark and twisted; luckily his wife and daughter found them entertaining. Mike is a member of the New England Horror Writers and lives outside Boston, Massachusetts. When he isn't writing or editing films, he is chasing down the plot for his next new story. His stories have anchored multiple anthologies including Dark Speculations Vol. 1: Tales of Various Shapes and Shadows from Little Red Bird Publishing, If I Die Before I Wake Volume 6: Tales of the Dark Deep from Sinister Smile Press, and Stories We Tell After Midnight, Vol.2 from Crone Girls Press. Mike has also published Dogs, a horror novella, in 2022 through Muddy Paw Press.

IV

Anticipating Ruins

By: Lucretia Stanhope

Anticipating Ruins

Grace never expected silence to weigh so heavily underground, where air felt thick and still, untouched by the wind's caress. She and her team descended beneath the limestone cliffs two hours ago, but now hours felt more like weeks, maybe years, while trapped beneath the earth's skin. Forgotten ruins stretched before her, a labyrinth of crumbling stone and half-buried arches. Roots — pale, dead things — hung from the cavern's ceiling like limp fingers stretching toward the ground.

Their guides had abandoned them inside the cavern, muttering about cursed grounds and how no light ever touched these hollows. Grace hadn't believed their rambling warnings, not at first. But now, as her flashlight flickered, barely cutting through the dimness, a growing discomfort gnawed at her insides. There was something wrong with this place.

They shouldn't have come.

"Look at this."

Callum's voice sounded brittle in the cavern's heavy air. His flashlight beam swept over a towering column half-sunk into the earth, etched with symbols that hurt to look at. Geometric patterns twisted, and the more Grace stared, the more each pattern seemed to shift. It was as though the patterns weren't carved in stone but drawn in smoke, moving just out of focus.

"What is this place?" she whispered, more to herself than to anyone else.

Callum didn't answer. He focused his attention solely on tracing the symbols with his fingers. His breath came in shallow gasps, his eyes wide and swimming with a blend of fascination and fear.

The ruins moved around them, not physically, but in a way mirroring how shadows moved at the edges of peripheral vision.

Grace blinked. An arch that she was certain had been ten paces ahead now stood right in front of her. Crumbled stones were covered in thick, oily moss. It seemed ancient, but not in the same way surface ruins were ancient. This arch felt older, untouched by human memory.

"Let's go back," Sarah said, her voice thin and trembling. "We've seen enough."

Grace wanted to agree and pull them all back. But Sarah was always a little fast to panic in the field. That, and some force or instinct she couldn't explain kept her from following through. Her legs felt leaden, rooted in place by the oppressive weight of the space around them. An invisible force pulled at her, from deep in the earth, drawing her to journey further into the ruins.

"The guides said no one's been this deep." Callum's voice dropped to an almost reverent whisper. "Whatever this place was, it's been forgotten for millennia."

He knelt before a statue among a row of sculptures lining the passage.

Grace watched as studied the statue. He fed on this type of thing. Undiscovered, lost ancient history.

The figure had a humanoid appearance in some ways, but

the creature it immortalized in stone was far from human. Too many arms. Too many eyes. The statue's face was a grotesque mix of cultures that shouldn't have existed together — Mesoamerican and Egyptian, Byzantine and prehistoric. Stone melded together from disparate parts like a monster given life in some surreal dream.

All of the eyes on the statue flickered, shifting to meet Grace's own.

Something slithered in the dark, just beyond the reach of their lights. A cold shiver ran down Grace's spine, and she turned sharply, shining her light toward the sound. Nothing —just tangled roots hanging like a curtain.

Except one twitched.

She stepped closer, her heart thudding in her ears. The root wasn't a root. It was a hand —thin and emaciated, fingers webbed with rotting skin — slowly retreating into the cracks between stones. Grace froze, her throat tightening. It had been watching them.

"Did you see that?" she whispered.

No answer.

"Callum?"

Grace turned. Callum had vanished. Her eyes immediately slid over to Sarah.

Sarah's flashlight beam frantically danced across the stones.

"Where — where did he go?" Panic filled her voice.

The same sense of panic flared even more inside of Grace. The cavern felt too big now, like it had swallowed him whole. Ruins were rearranging themselves like a living maze, trapping them in twisting and turning passages. Grace rushed forward, following the faint impression Callum's footsteps left in the dust. Her search quickly turned useless. The longer she tried to follow his trail, the more the path shifted underfoot.

These ruins were alive.

Grace felt their life energy woven into the stones, in the way the walls pulsed, their surfaces slick with sweat. The statues, once distant, now crowded narrow corridors and leaned in, their twisted faces leering as though mocking her. Their eyes bulged, carved mouths stretched wide in silent laughter. Callum called out to Grace and Sarah. His voice sounded distorted, like he was trapped underwater. Grace sprinted forward, trying to close the gap between her and his voice. The distance never shortened no matter how fast she ran. Callum seemed to be continually ahead of her, perpetually just out of reach.

She stopped, chest heaving, and turned to Sarah.

Sarah stood frozen and stared at one of the statues, her eyes wide and mouth slack. Many arms stretched toward her, fingers brushing her skin.

Grace raced back to her friend, and reached out to pull her away, but Sarah's scream ripped through the cavern before she closed the gap between them.

What came from Sarah's mouth was no human scream — it mimicked the sound of something breaking, of sanity fracturing. Her body convulsed. All of Sarah's limbs jerked as though invisible hands were pulling her apart. Her face twisted, contorting with some unseen horror. The statue was moving now, its stone face cracking open to reveal a black and dripping substance beneath the surface. Sarah was forcefully pulled closer to the statue.

Her body folded, and Grace screamed her name as she finally reached Sarah. She grabbed her wrist, but trying to rip Sarah away from the statue was like trying to pull against the tide.

Her skin felt cold, too cold, and then she was gone — folded into the statue's belly as though she'd never existed.

Grace stumbled back, shaking, bile rising in her throat.

The statues were alive. The ruins, the architecture — none were relics of a dead civilization. None of it had been abandoned. The ancient civilizations that had built these objects, or perhaps *become* them, had never truly left. They were still here, beneath the earth, waiting.

Something rustled behind her.

Slow, deliberate footsteps, but not from Callum. The sound they made was too heavy and too calculated to be human. Grace's flashlight beam swept across the stones, her hand trembling, and landed on a figure at the far end of the hall.

It wasn't human.

The creature exposed by the light was enormous and towering. It possessed melted features of all the statues—a mosaic of different eras and different cultures found in its body. It dragged long and spindly arms across the ground. An unnaturally wide mouth, filled with jagged teeth seemingly carved from stone, gaped at her. Hundreds of eyes blinked in and out of existence as though the creature's face couldn't decide what shape it wanted to take.

It was walking toward her. No, *gliding.* Stones shifted beneath each foot, becoming part of the creature's movement. This was the ruins. It *was* a hidden and forgotten civilization.

Grace stumbled back, heart hammering, but her feet were no longer planted on solid ground. They sank into soft, bubbling earth. The cavern floor itself had become organic — a living entity. The roots weren't roots anymore. They were *bones,* pressing up through the earth. These were exposed remains of those who had come before, the dreamers who had wandered too far into the dark.

The walls closed in, statues leaning forward, mouths open ready to consume her.

Grace despaired at her legs being swallowed by living soil, preventing her escape. Even if she waded through earth back down the corridor, the labyrinth had no exit. And as the creature neared, she saw a frightening truth expressed in its many eyes — *there had never been a way out.*

The civilizations beneath the earth were never lost.

Grace felt the weight of the ruins pressing down on her. No air was left for her to scream. The statues whispered now, their voices soft and cold, snaking into her mind with words she should not understand. She stumbled back, eyes wide, and saw her hands—*no longer her hands.* Her fingers were becoming the color of stone, her veins tangled like the roots hanging from the ceiling, spreading across her skin, lacing up her arms.

She sank to her knees as a dull warmth began to spread from her chest, a fever that made the world around her blur. Grace's heartbeat slowed, throbbing to match the pulse of the ruins. Her skin tightened, cracked, as though some ancient dust beneath the surface had taken hold of her flesh.

The statues leaned closer, mouths unmoving, but their thoughts were as clear as spoken words.

You are home. You were always meant to return.

The ground beneath her trembled as the enormous figure in the distance — *the entity, the god of this place* — grew closer. A shifting mosaic of faces, eyes swallowing the light, and a mouth filled with jagged stones that glistened like wet bone, settled squarely on her. And then Grace understood.

She was not the first.

Callum and Sarah, along with nameless ones before them,

were all part of the cycle. Her eyes fell on apparitions of these people, emerging from the walls. Their faces were frozen in agonized expressions, their bodies woven into the architecture. They weren't dead. Not truly. They had *become* the ruins, still conscious, still aware, trapped in stone for eternity.

And she would join their ranks.

Her skin crumbled at the touch of the air, flakes of her body swirling in dim light like ash. Grace tried to move again, but her bones were growing heavy, fusing with ancient stone beneath her feet. Every breath tasted of dust and rot. Her vision narrowed as statues around her came alive, their mouths stretching open in silent screams.

The god-thing in the distance — so close now — bent down. It opened its cavernous mouth, a void filled with endless teeth, and *consumed her*.

Grace's mind stretched, thin and elastic, into the fabric of the ruins. Her body merged with the stones. Her bones became part of crumbling columns. Her thoughts, though faint, echoed through the tunnels, mingling with other voices belonging to those who had come before her.

She had become part of them now, another forgotten soul in a forgotten civilization, lost beneath the earth.

And the ruins waited in silent anticipation for the next one to stumble into the cavern.

Lucretia Stanhope hails from a small Kansas town where cornfields replace malls and there's not a stoplight in sight. She's a neurodiverse, relentlessly optimistic chronic illness warrior, navigating life's challenges with more grit than grace. Writing both prose and poetry, she blends fantasy, horror, and sci-fi with macabre glee, drawing inspiration from Edgar Allan Poe, Lewis Carroll, and Shel Silverstein. When not immersed in her stories, she dotes on her three rescue chihuahuas and her endlessly patient husband. Her stories have appeared in Flames Trees Press, Sudden Fictions podcast, and numerous anthologies including KJK's Collected Christmas IV and Potter's Field 8.

V

Edge Mountain Hello

By: R.E. Dyer

Edge Mountain Hello

Martin Tracer hugged his elbows and looked away, his eyes following the path of dry leaves skittering across the parking lot. Warmth enveloped him where he stood, but his insides shivered as if the relentless January wind stirring those leaves also buffeted him inside the waiting room.

Dr. Zhao held her clipboard against her chest and waited.

"If we know where this is headed …" Martin paused and found himself grasping for words. It was an impossible question to ask, but he had started. Nowhere to go but forward. "That there's no chance of recovery … and the pain will only get worse … for *her* …"

Martin forced himself to pull his eyes away from the frozen, cartwheeling leaves — more victims of this snowless, gray winter — and face the doctor. Her eyes bored into him and he finished in a rush.

"Wouldn't it be better to end things now?"

Dr. Zhao let a moment of silence draw out between them. She may have been searching for a polite response, but he suspected she was letting him feel the damning weight of his words.

"Mr. Tracer, there will come a time when the correct course

of action is to sedate Emily," she said. "Then nature will take its course. But today your wife can hear you and would appreciate your company."

Martin nodded, a spasmic reaction that elicited no further response from the doctor. He collapsed into a nearby seat and buried his face in his hands. Out of nowhere, tears flooded his eyes. Enough spilled down his cheeks to sneak past his lips and drench his mouth with their salty flavor. Dr. Zhao's shoes clicked a departing rhythm across the floor.

When Martin stood, he didn't return to Emily's room. He needed to spend time with his wife, but the woman lying in Room 318 bore no resemblance to the person he had married. Not just on the surface, although her yellow, clammy skin with patches of blue-red lace frightened him. The anger infecting her discolored eyes above the breathing tube cut so much deeper.

The hospital doors slid open, and the frigid air instantly wrapped uncaring fingers around Martin's lungs and squeezed. He stopped, shivering all over, and let out a violent cough. How close did this feel to Emily's every attempt to breathe? He inhaled, his chest filling with icy wisps, and hurried to his minivan — *their* minivan, he corrected, but an insidious voice whispered that soon it would be his alone. With his head ducked behind a sheltering arm, it took two tries to find the handle and jerk open the door.

Dropping into the driver's seat, he found himself staring east, toward Edge Mountain. He sat unmoving for twenty minutes, remembering Emily along the uneven mountain trails, full of life, setting the pace as she hopped fearlessly from one shifting rock to the next, and then started the car. Martin felt as if he'd received a message from the universe, or God — or maybe his desperate id just wanted to get the hell away from the hospital. He would find Emily up there, at the end of the North Lookout Trail, a place where she had always been happy.

Up there, he thought. *That's where she is.*

Martin left the hospital behind but convinced himself he was not abandoning Emily. He was driving *towards* her in every way that mattered.

* * *

A weathered wooden sign marked the entrance to Edge Mountain Hawk Sanctuary. One lone car occupied the lot, belonging to an employee who would be ending their shift in the visitor's center soon.

Martin cut the engine and suppressed a groan. He'd miscalculated the trip. Shadows were merging around the trailhead, heralding the advent of night. Sitting there, listening to the tick of the minivan's cooling engine, he felt less like a man on a quest to find his wife and more like an animal who had wandered into the crosshairs of a hunter's rifle. He imagined furtive movements among the trees ahead of him. A single thought crossed his mind, so clear he might have spoken it aloud: *This was a mistake.*

Go home, he thought. *Back to the hospital. Anywhere but here.*

His own laugh, dry and bitter, startled him. Martin rubbed his hands across his cheeks and shook his head. This place was *their* place. It belonged to him and Emily. He'd be damned before he scared himself out of taking solace in the fond memories they'd created together and left along the trail.

Shoving open the door, he hauled himself out, then reached back for his scarf and gloves. He stood, and a sudden gust slammed the door with a gunshot report.

What are you doing here?

Martin didn't possess an answer to that question. All he had was a direction, and that was the closest thing to a real answer he'd had in months. Trundling past the visitor's center and up the North Lookout Trail, he wound his scarf over his mouth and nose and tugged up his hood. The sharp wind brought blood to his thighs, which were covered by a single thin layer of denim. He kept his eyes forward.

The biting cold had sent everyone else home. He walked alone, feeling like a ghost wandering among slumbering trees and rustling brown grass. Undertaking such a rigorous climb brought on a sheen of sweat across his upper body, but pulling down his hood would only invite the full brunt of the mountain wind.

The heat is good, he remembered Emily telling him. *Sometimes you feel hot if you're too cold. Emergency services have found people naked up here, because hypothermia made them think they were burning up.*

"So we're not getting naked on the trail," Martin said into his scarf, remembering how his comment drew a single quirked eyebrow and a crooked grin. Up here, Em had been a different person.

Another blast across the mountain stole his breath, and with it came the memory of something else Emily used to say: "Windy days are the best for seeing hawks."

He wouldn't see much today, maybe a red-tail. By January, virtually all the hawks around here had settled into hidden places where they intended to spend the winter.

"Martin..."

The sound — *had there been a sound?* — brought him to a halt.

He spun around, craning his neck, first looking behind him along the trail, then peering into the forest in all directions. With the sun hugging the horizon, his visibility was limited to the nearest dozen or so trees. For a long while he stood, staring, waiting.

Nothing, he told himself. Only a combination of wind and scarf fabric against his ears, combined with the sense that he stood alone on top of a mountain. Alone and lonely.

Martin forced his eyes shut. Emily's smile rushed back to him. She always bounced on the balls of her feet at the edge of the lookout, as if her joy would cancel out gravity and keep her aloft if she slipped. Memories of the way they kissed on the rare event they were the day's last visitors also returned anew. Each image tore open a fresh wound. Pressure built behind his eyes, spreading toward the crown of his head.

Just go home, he thought.

Martin resisted the persistent internal demand to abandon this hike. He had almost reached the North Lookout. Their spot. With the owl, and the Horizon Trail, and her dreams of the Appalachian Trail. Martin cast one more wary glance behind him, assuring himself no one followed. Almost convinced, he faced north and walked.

* * *

Sullen thoughts ruled Martin. His mind replayed the day Dr. Zhao assured them his smoking could not be identified as the direct cause of Emily's sickness. *Could not be identified,* of course, was much different from, *you didn't do it.* He knew it and so did Emily and, as the fist squeezing her chest clenched tighter, so did her belief that one of his setbacks had turned into the proverbial straw that broke the camel's back.

The fateful One Thing Too Many.

Fresh tears conquered his eyes by the time Martin reached the North Lookout. He stopped at the trail's end and wiped them away with the back of his glove. His eyelashes crunched. A collection of rocks, some for stepping on, larger ones for sitting, stretched thirty yards along the peak of Edge Mountain. During migratory seasons, dozens of people crowded this spot — families, some with binoculars, others looking into the sky and pointing. Today, only the owl greeted his gaze.

Hand carved, perhaps by some long-ago Eagle Scout, the owl perched atop a thorny, twenty-foot wooden pole. At one time it had been mottled russet and white, but now only a barest hint of color remained around its graven eyes. The owl stared west, eyes seemingly following the setting sun. Martin had intended to greet the owl with a wave and enthusiastic hello the way Emily always had, like a childhood friend. Instead, he craned his neck in silence, exhaling into his scarf. The feeling of dread gripping him in the parking lot charged up the Lookout Trail like some wrathful phantom and enveloped Martin again. His heart hammered, shaking his chest.

Martin lowered his gaze, waiting for panic to subside. The owl had been Emily's friend, a companion she had looked forward to seeing on childhood visits long before she met him. It had been foolish to expect the sight of the avian totem to bring him respite.

He finally stumbled away, rubbing his aching head through his hood. A shuddering sigh worked free from his lips as he settled on the far edge of the lookout. His feet dangled fifteen hundred feet above the valley floor. Treetops waved like the tips of brandished spears below him, and a strong breeze pounded his back. The tiniest sliver of moon hung in the northeast, faint stars pebbling the surrounding cloudless sky.

The wind whispered. His mind was blank.

Martin studied his right wrist. Those scabs had flaked away now, but white lines served as silent reminders of the last time he tried to hold Emily's hand. She struck quickly, raking sharp nails across his flesh. It had also been the last time he saw pleasure in her eyes.

Movement caught his attention, and he looked up to see a dark shape plunge out of the sky and vanish among the trees. Whatever it was had been too large and ungainly to be a red-tailed hawk. A shiver, unrelated to the icy air, raced along his spine.

Just a hawk, Martin told himself. Because what he saw couldn't have been what he thought he saw.

He sat there, waiting for its return, perhaps gripping a meal in curving talons, wondering when he'd become so easily freaked out. Except, he admitted, he was sitting on a deserted mountaintop at sunset. In January. And the wooden owl stood there on its perch, judging him. He couldn't forget the damn owl.

Sweat trickled into Martin's ear and he yanked down his hood, preferring the wind to basting inside his coat. Mountain gusts tugged at his hair, raked across his slick forehead.

A despairing hunger awakened within him, a craving for a fond memory before darkness chased him back to the daily nightmare of the hospital. He stared at the far side of the lookout, beyond the owl. Below laid the Horizon Trail, invisible from where he sat looking. Emily had wanted to hike it with him someday, follow it all the way out to the Appalachian Trail. Martin had wanted to do it for her, but she knew he didn't want to go, so she never pressed him to do it.

Years ago, the first time they came, Martin had believed the North Lookout was the top of a cliff, straight down in every direction but back. He didn't realize the west side had a gentler slope until the hiker's arm came over the edge from the Horizon Trail. If Emily hadn't seen his expression and burst into laughter, he would have screamed.

For the first time in days, Martin felt a genuine smile tug at the corners of his mouth.

There, he thought. *That's your positive note to end the visit.*

He started to rise, and a moan reached his ears.

Martin hesitated only a moment before racing to the lookout's western edge. His breath escaped in short, hot gasps. A three-foot drop led to a narrow stone outcropping, the first of many steps winding down and out of sight. Trail maps marked the Horizon in red: steep and rocky.

He tugged off a glove and clawed down his scarf, sucking in gulps of frozen air and, in his fear, relishing them. He tried to replace the glove with shaking hands, and it slipped, skipping down the rough hewn steps. He listened to the *tik ... tik* as it went and prayed his imagination had misinterpreted a lonely animal's call.

Martin leaned over the edge. On his right, cloying mists rose from the valley and glittered in starlight. Maybe the ground wasn't fifteen hundred feet from this spot, but he wouldn't feel the difference if he fell.

He clenched his jaw, eyes wide as he strained to hear.

There. The sound prickled his scalp. What felt like a bowling ball dropped into the pit of his stomach. He knew that voice. And she had said his name.

Martin glanced back at the visitor's center and its lone

attendant. A public phone was inside the center, but the trail head lay a mile away from him. There was no time. Uselessly, he checked his cell to confirm his phone had no signal above the sanctuary.

What he heard lingered in his ears like an echo. Gooseflesh broke out in a rash across his sweat-drenched body. He dropped on hands and knees and lowered his legs to the first step. Getting back up would require climbing. He didn't think the drop was that far down, but when his feet settled, the ground of the North Lookout reached his armpits. He didn't waste time wondering about the return trip. He leapt from stone to stone, clinging to the cliff in a way he knew would make experienced hikers laugh — but each step was narrow and slick and, down here, the sun had set.

He reached the bottom. It struck him that he stood on the Horizon Trail. Emily's dream. The gnarled trunks of oak trees — some chestnut, others northern red — rose above him. Clots of brown leaves blocked the light except for an occasional, errant beam.

Martin stepped forward and studied the trail, readying himself to find the voice if she spoke again. He sensed how preposterous this situation would appear to an outside observer — thinking a lone woman on Edge Mountain might have seen him peering over the trailhead and called out for help. But Martin's imagination went beyond the absurd, fixating on a single, mad idea. With each passing moment he became more convinced that the short, stifled sounds had been in Emily's voice.

A snowflake struck his exposed forehead. He swiped it away with his bare right hand. Instead of shivering out of control, the exertion of his frantic descent had raised his internal thermometer by a couple of extra degrees.

"Martin."

Her voice banished all thoughts of improbability. It *was* Emily.

He opened his mouth to say her name, but no words escaped his tongue. Not far off, a gray form separated from indistinct shadows.

She emerged next to a pool of starlight, dressed in an oversized hospital gown that hung over her stooped shoulders. White slippers left her skeletal ankles and calves exposed. She clung to an IV pole like a wizened sorceress clutching her staff, one cheek resting against its polished metal shaft, so still that none of the drip bags swayed. The flesh around her mouth had turned a raw pink where tape had secured her now-absent breathing tube.

Martin stumbled back.

Not her.

He realized the notion of his wife as two different people — Emily Before and Emily Now— had taken on concrete reality within his mind. The present-day, dying version of Emily could not be here. Impossible. But he could not deny what was before his eyes.

Tears glistened on her cheeks. At first, he mistook them for melted snowflakes. Then he heard her ragged, shallow sob. Pain gripped her with cruel talons. A strangled cry rose in Martin's throat, and he reached out to her.

"Em," he said.

Her eyes opened at the sound of her name. She stepped into the light, revealing her skin bore a marigold hue. Worse were her eyes — perfectly round and gleaming amber, with pupils the size of nickels.

Owl's eyes.

She stepped closer and his shoes slid on a slippery patch where there had been dry ground. Leaves blackened and drifted down from branches now bowing under the weight of hardening icicles.

Martin's shoes gained traction. He ran for the steps, not daring to look back. The wheels on her IV pole screeched while rolling over freezing earth. A wooden pop behind him filled his mind with a distinct image of a fallen log bursting. Her wet, hitching moan echoed off bushes, trees, and the face of Edge Mountain itself.

He reached the end of the trail and climbed, ignoring patches of new frost. He would rather slip and plummet to the valley floor than be caught by whatever his wife had become. Protruding rocks scraped the flesh of his bare hand, but his remaining glove proved too bulky to grasp and pull. Halfway up, he bit down on the polyester shell above his middle finger and tugged it off. He continued onward, grabbing at slippery rocks with both hands.

His foot came down on the last step. Martin threw his arms onto the surface of the North Lookout. At eye level, ice-encrusted stones shone like earthbound stars. He filled his hands with them and jumped, shoes scrabbling against the cliffside. The stone under his right hand rolled, and his stomach lurched as he hung, weightless, over the valley.

A waxy hand, so cold it burned, caught him by the wrist and hauled him up. He came down hard on his back. His head crashed against unyielding stone. The sky spun, then blurred.

* * *

I've got you."

His eyes flitted behind closed lids at Emily's delicate whisper. It had been *so long*.

She straddled him the way she used to, when they made love, and his body reacted. Warmth bloomed, and she bent over him, radiating heat. Martin struggled to catch his breath, so he mouthed her name. He unzipped his heavy winter coat, and her hands traced paths along his chest.

Where she touched, trails of fire. Martin tried to moan, but it caught in his throat. His back arched to meet her, and she dug her heels into the backs of his knees to grind against him. She dragged her hands down his sides, and he burned. He tugged at his shirt in desperation.

Em! he tried to say. Pressure built inside his head and his chest. His mouth gaped, and she pressed harder against him. Her touch was fire.

Pleasure erupted into a torturous flame and the pleasant dream ended. Martin's eyes drifted open to see her hovering there, predator gaze staring down, raw lips curved in a lustful smile.

Her hands plunged onto his bare chest; one palm pressed flat above each lung. She did not let go. He couldn't inhale to scream, so she shrieked for him. Martin's eyes rolled, reaching, straining. His fingers straightened till the knuckles popped like firecrackers in their sockets. Darkness crept in, narrowing his vision. The last image greeting his eyes was the top of the pole rising above the North Lookout.

The owl — Emily's owl — was gone.

R.E. Dyer's other eerie tales and supernatural yarns can be found in the anthologies "Dolls in the Attic" from Terrorcore and "The Elemental Cycle" from Eerie River Publishing, and the magazines Fraidy Cat Quarterly and Dungeon. A former teacher, trainer, and curriculum developer, he does his writing in the wilds of Pennsylvania, where he lives at the whim of a large cat with his wife and two children. Find him at redyerauthor.com

VI

Containment Protocols

By: Aaron Frale

Containment Protocols

Tara woke with the smell invading her senses as if it was still happening. Her mother's burnt flesh. The way her hair seemed to melt. The scream still echoed in her mind. She could never forget.

"Mommy."

A soft voice thrust Tara to full consciousness. An astral axe formed over a small silhouette in the shadows by her bedside. Tara realized at the last moment what she was doing and let the psychic energy dissipate. The weapon disappeared, not that Maxi would have been able to see it. Psychic weaponry only appeared to people who were trained. Her progeny was seven.

"I had a nightmare, Mommy."

"Let's go back to bed and do meditation."

Tara developed the ritual for a child with an overactive mind. She forced herself out of bed and ushered Maxi out the door. On the way to the bedroom, she asked about the dreams and assured her daughter that what she saw and heard amid her slumber wasn't real. Except it was. Maxi had been there too.

Once Maxi was asleep again, Tara ventured back into her room and saw the time. 4 am. Too early to be awake, too late to fall asleep. She turned on her bedside lamp, so as not to wake her snoring husband, and glanced over at her uniform, trench coat and fedora.

* * *

Despite arriving at work early, Tara's Personal Assistant, a soft-spoken man named Lawrence, already had her quadruple shot Americano with sugar-free vanilla syrup and a light dollop of heavy cream waiting on her desk. It was piping hot, just how she liked it. A lower-level Paranormal Investigator sporting polished shoes, crisp trench coat, and immaculate fedora stood at attention when she entered her office, as if she was the commanding officer of the US armed forces.

"You need to make a decision on Haiti," Lawrence said, swiping information onto Tara's tablet.

"Let the Sales Associates handle it."

"The dracofarnekar is causing havoc after the earthquake. There's already two perms."

"All the reason Sales should up their game," Tara said and fell into her chair. "We can't baby them every time something goes wrong. What about the other incidents?"

"Tokyo is secure, Janitorial is on cleanup. The Brightford Township needs reinforcements. Congo and New Hampshire are in information gathering. Three more quests were accepted by our Branch last night and a fourth was taken by IT."

"IT?"

"Some fool has an idea to study the monsters."

"Could be useful, but dangerous. Flag that employee." Tara nodded to the PI standing at attention near the entry of her office. "Mind telling me what Captain Freedom is doing there?"

"Captain America," Lawrence corrected her.

"Whatever." Tara beckoned her over. "You better have a good

reason for interrupting my morning coffee."

"Cassidy West." The woman extended her hand. She reminded Tara of an actress who starred in just about every romantic comedy she had seen. Tara couldn't name the actress off the top of her head, but Cassidy was her doppelganger.

Tara did not reciprocate the handshake. Until she knew this Cassidy a little better, it was best not to get too friendly. Her underlings needed to follow her orders, not like her. Cassidy stood next to the chair facing Tara's desk, waiting for her lead.

At least she was aware of protocol. Tara motioned her to sit down.

"There's a cure for the grutomaton virus," Cassidy blurted out after taking a seat.

Tara narrowed her eyes.

"This better not be a prank or I'll feed you to the dragon myself."

"I wouldn't mind round 2 with the dragon."

Tara now realized what sparked the hint of recognition from meeting Cassidy. It wasn't her uncanny resemblance to a certain movie star. No, it was the fact that she was one of the few to pass the 4-minute mark with the dragon. Cassidy was making a name for herself as she climbed the PI ranks.

Tara would have to be careful with her, the most ambitious were also the most trouble.

"What's this cure?" She asked.

"Not what, but where. It's, well, I don't know if everyone here has the right permissions."

"Leave the room. Lawrence."

"Yes, ma'am," he said and scurried out. He was a credit to the Personal Assistant Branch, an invisible yet vital part of the company.

Once the door closed, Cassidy picked up where she left off earlier.

"Dimension 597014340B-871146001C has …"

Tara's face grew pale.

"What do you know about that dimension?" she snapped.

"I was there."

"Then you know why it's off limits."

"But there could be a —"

"No personnel are allowed in or out," Tara said. "Let me be clear. If you go there, no matter what you find. It will be the end of your career if you are even allowed back in."

"But."

"You have my final answer. You are not authorized for transit."

"But this could …"

"Would you like to spend the rest of your time at the company as a Worker?"

"My talents are better suited here, and once you choose a class —"

"One word from me." Tara stared eye to eye with growing intensity. "And I will cut off your training, not just for the PIs but any Branch. You'll be PI in all but name only. You will never progress in skills, and your tier will stagnate. Soon, you will be stuck doing menial labor until you keel over from exhaustion. Am I clear?"

Cassidy's expression darkened.

"Crystal."

"Good," Tara said. "Tell Lawerence to come back inside on your way out."

Cassidy turned and, without saying another word, stormed out of her office.

* * *

Tara got a late-night ping in her tracking system long after Lawrence had retired to his sleeping pod. Cassidy was awake and requested an elevator. Tara cursed and pressed a button under her desk. A panel on her wall opened and slid aside, revealing a combination of firearms and medieval weaponry.

She grabbed a morning star, two swords, and two pistols with glowing ammo. They all shrunk and disappeared into a pocket on the interior of her trench coat. Tara opened an adjacent drawer, hidden in the wall, that held a black bodysuit. It captured the light so thoroughly that the bodysuit resembled a cartoon hole an unsuspecting toon would fall into if they weren't careful.

After dressing, she waved her hand over a wall decorated with a painting of a rickety sailing ship in a tumultuous sea. The panel and picture disappeared, and an elevator door materialized in their place. Tara hit the call button, and it opened immediately to reveal an elevator car modeled on a 1980s casino lift. She stepped inside.

The elevator housed a single button. She placed her finger on the button, and hesitated, before finally drawing a deep breath and pressing it

"Home."

After a brief high-speed lurch, the door opened. Daylight flooded the new location, blinding her for a moment. Once her vision adjusted, she could see the decimation.

The room in front of her was completely burnt. Office equipment was nothing more than crisp husks and melted plastic. Cubicle walls sagged like ice cream on a hot day. Corpses were piled near the elevator door, people desperate to get out before security protocols cleaned the infection.

Tara had a flash of her mother, skin boiling, last words frozen on her lips. Her chest tightened, and she leaned against the wall. Panic creeped into her body until she choked and nearly tore off her bodysuit that now felt too tight around her neck.

She heard a grunt in the distance, and then a shout.

Tara snapped herself out of her panic attack and ran toward the noise. Burnt flesh around her assaulted her nostrils. She wanted to puke but pushed herself forward. While she ran, she pulled the morning star from her pocket, and it grew back into a full-sized weapon.

The scream turned to cursing and was joined by sounds of battle. She charged through the husk of an office until she rounded a corner. At the opposite side of the massive room, Cassidy was locked into battle with a fierce monster that was equal parts copy machine and creature. Tara pushed hard to close the gap.

Bloodshot eyes bulged where the display should have been. Yellow stained teeth had sprouted from the center, and crablike legs burst from the bottom. It was an absurd mix of creature and copier, but deadly and enraged. Cassidy grappled with it. The thing had already taken a large chunk from her thigh, the flesh dripping from the maw.

The young PI had a saber and barely fended off blows from the beast. She also peppered green astral arrows in its hide that blended muscle and plastic. It charged and rammed into Cassidy and bowled her over, even as she landed a blow that gouged one of the beast's eyes and embedded more projectiles in its body. The collision knocked Cassidy off her feet and the creature clamped onto her sword arm.

As soon as Tara was in range, she summoned a titanic amount

of psychic energy. A beam of light opened in the ceiling and, a glowing angel appeared and descended from the heavens. The divine being was cut from the Greek gods themselves and held a flaming sword. Both wings shimmered with the light of ten thousand suns. With one swipe from its mythic blade, the angel sliced the creature in half.

The angel dissipated almost as fast as it appeared, and the gruesome mix of blood, organic and machine parts twitched a final time. Cassidy had fallen unconscious tangled in the mess of the thing, her life force draining out from the wounds inflicted by the fight. Tara placed her hands on the damaged leg first and concentrated.

Astral arms reached out from her body while her hands never moved. The ghostly limbs dug into the young PI's body and found a severed artery. She stitched it together again and did the same with the muscle tissue and then the skin.

After healing the leg, Tara used the same approach to bind wounds in the arm and shoulder. Good enough to make Cassidy's mangled hand functional again and stop the bleeding, but not enough to allow her to start fighting again. Unless Cassidy had any skills in off handed combat, she would have to rely on psychic attacks alone until she could get proper healing.

Tara reached into another pocket in her coat and withdrew a vial that instantly grew to full size. She forced a foul concoction down the woman's throat. Cassidy gagged and choked, but Tara held the woman's mouth closed until she swallowed. All the blood the young PI had lost would soon be restored.

When Cassidy's eyes opened a few moments later, it was already too late. Another photocopier creature had rounded the corner. Only this time, it was not alone. An entire pack raced toward the two women, with smaller desk sized printers nipping at their feet. A feral vending machine and two frenzied industrial sized washers brought up the rear.

This mob of mutated, sentient office equipment blocked the escape path to the elevator. The creatures charged, and Tara sent a wave of psychic energy that knocked the entire group back. She hoisted the dazed Cassidy on her shoulder as other creatures flooded past the first group. Tara sent another burst knocking them back while the first were recovering and a third group rounded the corner.

It was happening all over again.

When her world fell the first time, anything with a microchip had transformed like a werewolf under a full moon. Formerly inanimate office equipment morphed into something deadly and bestial. Billions had died in the first few seconds of the outbreak, billions more within minutes.

It happened so fast.

Tara's family mostly survived only because they were within fighting distance of an elevator when chaos erupted across the globe, but not all made it. Her parents had almost reached the elevator door when the containment protocols triggered. Tara's husband had to hold her back while her brother shut the door. Everyone she had ever known was gone in a flash while her daughter sat screaming in the corner of the elevator.

Cassidy must have been a rookie at the time, not even a PI yet. Probably got lucky by being inside an elevator when the attack happened. A couple hundred people in total, that was it. Now the beasts claimed her homeworld, creatures that would forever rule the land. There was nothing for them here.

Tara created a barrier of psychic energy between her and the pack. The creatures charged the barrier and bounced off. Tara felt it beginning to falter. She dragged her underling deeper into the building, trying to remember where the next elevator shaft was located. It felt like trying to navigate a hometown after it had been bombed out in an air raid. She knew the building well, but the destruction was just enough to keep her guessing on which way to go.

She replaced her morning star with a sword because Cassidy was taking up her arm. A k-cup coffee machine with murderous eyes and spider legs crashed out of an office and sprayed scalding liquid. Tara used her coat to block the weaponized goop and sliced the thing in half with her sword.

She chopped, sliced, and thwacked her way through a maze of creatures who thankfully hadn't built to a horde level that would fell even the mightiest of PIs. When Tara reached an office with a name plaque she recognized, she kicked open the ajar door. The rumble of thousands of charging beasts echoed through the surrounding halls.

The containment protocols hadn't breached the interior of the office, and it was in surprisingly good condition, despite missing a computer, phone, paper shredder, or any other electronics that would have beasted out when the end came. Tara tossed her charge on a thick brown leather couch, shut the door, and pulled the blinds.

Cassidy's eyes registered improved awareness of her surroundings when Tara put her finger to her lips. The whole room shuttered from a massive rumble. A light bulb burst and a painting of a farmhouse fell from the wall. The pair waited in perfect silence while the horde passed. Once Tara was reasonably sure the vast majority were out of earshot, she turned her full attention to Cassidy.

"Come on, we are getting out of here."

"We can't," Cassidy said. "We have to find it."

"What?"

"There's a piece of equipment in this building, a fax machine, printer, computer monitor, something that's immune to the Grutomaton virus."

Her revelation gave Tara pause. She never heard of anything immune to the virus. There were outbreaks that would just infect a conference room or a call center, sometimes just the copy room, but every piece of equipment that came in contact with one of the creatures would turn. It was only a matter of time.

To believe something on this world was immune was a fantasy. That kind of wishful thinking got the young PIs killed. Tara had seen too much. The only way to stop the spreading virus was through the elevator shafts. Their rides wouldn't turn into beasts, even if fighting happened inside the elevator. No one knew why, or even how the elevator system worked, other than it did.

Maybe it was leftover technology from a multiverse spanning civilization or just as magical as something a person would find in a wizarding school. Even if some fabled piece of her home dimension still worked, a printer that would never jam, could she really bring it back to Earth?

When Tara was buffing up on Earth history, so she wouldn't feel like an idiot when she would get seemingly common facts wrong, she came across a story of Typhoid Mary. The story related how a cook carried the typhoid disease but never expressed any symptoms. She got her clients sick without even knowing what she was doing.

Was bringing back a piece of equipment immune to the Grutomaton virus worth the risk? Billions died the day her world fell. Would the artifact kill billions more when she brought it over? Did she want to risk the sacrifice of billions of people who lived on Earth because she couldn't sleep at night?

Tara was not only the defacto leader of the PIs but the highest-ranking member of the company, Tier 1.1. People either would do what she said, act because they thought it would please her, or emulate her because everyone knew her name. Even the people who painted her as someone to be reviled and feared were doing it because of her mere existence.

What she did and what she said would have consequences, whether she intended them or not. Her job was to make decisions that would harm the least amount of people, or the damage mitigated through Janitorial. The cure and downfall handed to her, and she wasn't sure if the sensation deep in her gut was only her trauma warping her ability to do what was best for Earth. The people she had sworn to protect.

"Where is it?" Tara asked.

"It's here," Cassidy said. "In this building. Accounting I think, maybe payroll."

"We're in HR right now," Tara motioned to the office around them. This simple fact had kept them alive as all HR offices had privacy shields that let nothing out – no sound, no light, not even smells. It offered the only place creatures couldn't find them, and the only reason they were alive. Her brother had worked in HR before he moved to Public Relations. The whole family was planning their next cruise when his computer went berserk.

Had it been even a few minutes later, her husband would have been taking Maxi to daycare and… no, she wouldn't let it happen again. She couldn't let it happen again.

Tara reached out with a tendril of psychic energy and put Cassidy into a sleeper hold.

"What are you doing?" the young PI managed to croak.

"You are going to take a ride in the nearest elevator," Tara said, as Cassidy's consciousness faded again. "I'm going to Accounting alone."

* * *

Tara crept through the hallways in her void-colored bodysuit. Her trench coat and fedora were left in the elevator with a note to Cassidy to have it dry cleaned and waiting in her office where the young PI would wait for her punishment. Even if Cassidy's tip turned out to be true, she couldn't let indiscretion go without consequences. Their homeworld was off limits for a reason. Even top-tier employees would have to rest sometime. Her psy wasn't an unlimited resource, and she had burned through a lot just to stay alive.

The Accounting Branch was a maze of tight hallways and offices. No large call center floors here like in some other public facing departments. When it came to people's books and taxes, they valued their privacy. This added danger to the journey because a grutomaton could hide in lots of places, but also didn't have many large rooms where they could assemble.

However, if a horde did show up, it would box her in. There would be no escape. She would be another one of the nameless bodies left to rot after the world collapsed. Her heart rate increased, and she tried to suppress it. She breathed deeply and practiced the meditation techniques that had gotten her through rough patches when the memories were too hard to bear.

She almost turned to the nearest elevator and ran, but her curiosity pushed her forward, looking for electronics that hadn't turned. Most offices were empty, the electronics beasting out long ago. There were shattered windows, signs of scuffle, and bodies.

Billions of people. Hundreds of survivors.

Tara thought seeing the corpses would give her immunity, help her process what happened. Perhaps even find comfort in knowing her parents weren't the only ones. But they were so close to making it. She could still feel the foul smell in her nostrils… the last moments of her mother.

The containment protocols hadn't triggered everywhere. Accounting was relatively untouched by the flames. A hall or an office got incinerated here and there but, for the most part, the building was left to decay in the same state it had been after all the people died. They were still in their suits, stained coffee cups on their desk, remnants of rotted breakfast sandwiches.

If the containment protocols had fully triggered, then a crater would occupy the spot where the building was and, perhaps, they could have come back to the world and tried to rebuild. However, some devices controlling the system beasted out, leaving entire floors fried and some untouched.

Tara rounded a corner and saw a light through the crack under a door. She turned up the stealth protocol of her void suit with a thought and blended into the shadows to become nothing more than a dark spot in an empty corridor. She crept up to the edge of the door and heard a peculiar noise.

A familiar sound, one she heard every day that usually blended into the background. It was a copy machine, spitting out copies. Lawrence used one down the hall from her office and she heard it if she left her door open and he didn't shut the one to the copy center. Such a mundane noise seemed out of place.

Who would be making copies on a dead world?

She could project her consciousness on the astral plane into the room and take a glance at what was going on, but it would leave her physical body vulnerable to attacks. Considering the grutomatons could strike at any moment, she didn't dare to leave her body behind.

Luckily, her conundrum resolved itself when a man stepped out with a bundle of copies fresh off the press. He looked ordinary in every way. Brown hair, yellow company shirt, and blue jeans. The only thing peculiar about him was a blood streak across his clothes that didn't look like his own, and two deep abysses for eyes. They were as black as her suit.

He whistled a tune and stopped when his eyes came to rest on her location.

"Can I help you with something?"

Tara was taken aback by his question. Ordinary people couldn't see her when she was in the suit. Extraordinary people would even have trouble noticing and brush her presence off as a figment of their imagination. This man was beyond either category.

She decided to play it nonchalantly. Anyone making copies in a world more hostile to humans than sunbathing on Mercury, was someone to take seriously.

"I heard a noise. Thought I'd come and investigate."

Tara came out of her crouch and took a few steps forward. She leaned against the wall like she was chatting with a coworker. Her sword hung limply, but not in a way where she couldn't slash or parry if needed.

The man shifted his copies to one hand and leaned against the wall with the same casual stance that still was ready for action. Tara could tell that he was a trained fighter, and well trained at that. His stance, the way he held his body was a person who wouldn't be caught flat footed. His yellow shirt denoting him as the lowest level employee of the company was only a disguise meant to mislead an opponent.

"Just making some copies."

His tone suggested this was basic water cooler talk. She glanced down at the pile of papers. The top page was emblazoned with a silhouette of a man wearing a top hat in the corner.

"Odd place to make them," she said.

"It doesn't jam."

"What?"

"The printer doesn't jam, so it doesn't beast out."

"Ah, I see. Still, a dangerous place to be."

"There's an elevator around the corner. I can take you there if you'd like."

He gestured toward the unseen elevator while flashing a smile that was disarming and insincere at the same time.

"If it's all the same," Tara said. "I'd like to see what's beyond that door."

The yellow-shirted man smiled and gestured for her to walk past him. From the ways his muscles tensed, Tara sensed she was in for a fight. Unfortunately, her suit's telepathic interface couldn't pull up any data about him. She couldn't even get a read on his level. Either she was about to fight someone so overpowered it would be no contest or she would end his life with a blow meant to incapacitate him. There was no way to tell which scenario was more likely.

Tara stepped forward as if she didn't have a care in the world. Right as she was about to go past him, her invisible psychic armor deflected a dagger aimed at her throat. He wasn't a psychic class, that was a small favor or else she'd be dead.

She stabbed him in the gut at almost the same moment she heard the rush of air signaling the dagger attack. Her blow connected to his gut, and Tara wrenched the sword to the side in a manner that would spill the intestines of any normal person. But nothing spilled out except an ooze as black as his eyes.

He kicked her in the side, and the force of the blow sent Tara through the wall into one of the derelict offices. He set down his papers neatly on the floor and cracked his knuckles as he walked towards her.

She hopped to her feet in one move and readied her sword. The yellow-shirt stepped through the opening her body had made, and she created a half dozen psychic axes that crashed down on him as soon as he reached the other side. They passed through him as if he wasn't there.

Just her luck. Psychic immunity, but that didn't mean she couldn't use it defensively. She reinforced the shield around her body and began to stir the air in the room. Objects began hurling their way towards her adversary, but he waved his hand, her shield and whirlwind dissipated.

With a flick of his wrist, her sword arm bent at an unnatural angle, and her weapon clattered to the ground. She used her good hand to pull an automatic pistol with plasma rounds for slugs that burned as hot as the heart of the sun.

Tara unloaded a clip, and black ooze spurted in buckets from the guy as he fell backward from the flurry of bullets. He lay motionless only for a moment then his eyes popped open again and he rose to his feet without bending his legs. It reminded her of a vampire rising from a coffin in a cheap horror movie. Tara gritted her teeth and wrapped the fingers of her broken hand around another pistol. She fired both pistols into him amid a tsunami of pain coursing through her body.

Tara didn't have time to mend her bones and the pistols were a distraction at best. as she would reload one while continuing to fire with the other. She'd eject the spent cartridge and slammed a new one that was forming to full size from her storage.

She was able to maneuver around the black ooze covered man, back through the hole in the wall and out into the hallway. The walls started to shake from a distant rumble. Glass on one of the doors shattered. The man in the yellow shirt stood motionless.

Tara didn't wait. She ran.

A colossal wave of grutomatons spilled into the hallways and charged her. Snarling printers, killer coffee machines, fluttering smart fans, and other creatures flooded the hallway out for her blood. Tara sprinted as the horde trampled each other and snapped at one another while they crashed towards her. The noise from the stampede drowned out everything else.

She risked a glance back as she turned a corner. The man in the yellow shirt stood in the center of the hall. Machines had parted ways to go around him. He smiled at her with that same empty grin.

Tara didn't skip a beat.

She ran.

* * *

Tara threw up in the bathroom at work. She slumped next to the toilet, tears streaking down her face. Her arm still ached a little from her trip back from her home dimension. While healing meant she would never spend more than a day recovering from a broken limb, some residual pain always lingered. Sometimes, something didn't grow back quite right or tissue took longer to heal.

She went back after a couple days with a properly equipped team rigidly following safety standards, but the printer was gone. The room had been scrubbed clean. No trace of the fabled printer immune to the grutomaton virus or anything else of value was left in the place. Even Tara's psychic powers that allowed her to delve into the area's history showed nothing. It was like the room was empty and had always been that way. Tara knew better. She'd heard the device. She saw the print outs.

She had almost terminated Cassidy for flagrant disregard of safety protocols, Fortunately, neither brought back the virus. Earth was safe for now. Tara went light on her by demoting Cassidy back to Tier 12 and assigning her job duties far beneath an average PI.

Once she was sure nothing was left in her stomach, she flushed the toilet and stood again. Tara left the stall and examined herself in the mirror. She breathed deep. Tara could do this. Her home was gone but not forgotten. She washed up and saw a note had been slipped under the bathroom door.

She picked up the flier. It had a brief message printed on it.

"The company lies. Find out the truth."

An email for more information was below the message. Tara noticed a silhouette of a man wearing a top hat.

On rare occasions, this author creature known as an Aaron Frale can be spotted in the wilds of Montana. This whimsical being screams and plays heavy metal guitar in the indie prog band, Spiral, and sometimes writes humorous fantasy novels. Oh no, he's spotted us. Get back in the jeep! Get back in —

You can further explore the world of Containment Protocols in the Office Maxi book collection at Aaron's official author page aaronfrale.com and also check out his other books series there.

VII

Holes

By: Michael Paige

Holes

Everything stops when the rifle goes off, when the jittery eye of the hunter finds the scope, curls a woeful finger around the trigger, and holds their breath for the thunder.

We'd been at it for days by that point, suited up in our camouflaged layers and hiking for miles through lodgepole pines until we settled on a fringe behind the tree line.

Pops made me wear one of his hunting caps since I refused to cut my hair before the trip.

This was my gift to him for his birthday — a promise that we'd go hunting in September together. He didn't want cake or presents. He just wanted to share his interest with me the same way his Pops did with him. Another hunter for the family line.

Seeing the excitement in his face, I didn't have the heart to tell him how much I didn't want to go. It wasn't like lining the perfect pellet on a row of bottles or shooting unsuspecting flies with rubber bands (*I was a real devil to them*), No, this was different — an impartial bullet moving at 2500 fps to rip another creature's breath away. No more thoughts. No more sunsets. Just a loud and sudden end.

We spotted the herd through binoculars the day before, heard their teasing bugles in the distance, but weren't close enough for a shot.

"Elk must be getting pressured," Pops said while I swatted a wasp away from my face. "Lucky for us, I think I have an idea where the gang is heading."

Creeping at a snail's pace, we moved quietly through the clearing, surrounded by tall, irritating weeds.

Suddenly, Pops stopped, bringing a finger up to his lips to hush me.

Do you see it?

The question formed silently on his lips while he pulled the rifle from his shoulder.

I looked past him beyond the thicket. Some form of dark mass moved along the forest floor. My adjusting eyes spied two branching antlers I initially mistook for tree limbs. A large bull elk, raking a tree about seventy yards.

I nodded back to Pops. We moved cautiously, mindful to not disturb any rock or sticks we crept over. I could see its blanketed tan fur connecting to a dark brown head. The bones protruding from its skull made me think of a crown with two ivory tridents. A beautiful creature. For a moment, I forgot why we were there. The elk's head bobbed as it scraped against the bark. To our left, two cow elk appeared out of the underbrush, investigating the scene.

The raking stopped as the bull's dark eyes scanned its surroundings. We were close enough to see excess snot blow out of its snout and a lump of muscle twitch on its back.

Pops handed me the rifle, silently whispering for me to take aim in my ear. I breathed into the weedy scrub around us, trying to focus through the scope. I thought of the field behind our house, where Pops had filled water bottles with blue food dye and set them up for target practice. "Exhale through your teeth and just before your lungs empty, pull the trigger." He'd whisper before every shot. I'll never forget the day when the stars aligned, and one bottle erupted in a spray of blue mist. I was real proud of hitting the bullseye, but shooting those blue bottles didn't stack very high compared to the real thing.

Pops lightly gripped my shoulder. "Breathe, boy. Breathe in, breathe out. Settle in. Let the last breath about half-way out, and when you're ready, pull."

I couldn't concentrate. Everything around us was too loud, too strenuous. Air fought to escape my lungs, but I held it back, letting pressure build in my chest like two balloons ready to pop.

"I can't do it." I hissed too loudly, gnashing my teeth together, fighting back tears starting to run. "I can't, I'm sorry, I can't …"

"It's alright." He said calmly, taking the gun away from me. Pops gently dug one of his knees into the ground and took position, his eye peering through the concealed casing of the scope and zeroing in on the quarry. With the butt of the rifle pressed against his shoulder and cheek squished firmly into the stock, he exhaled.

The crack from the gun broke the cover of silence and a bullet pegged right into the bull elk's hide. It leaped on its hind legs and dashed in a gallop through the trees, followed by the two other elk.

"Holy cow, did you see that shot?!" His eyes brimmed with excitement when he glanced at me.

We trailed after the elk, crossing over murky brooks and using blemishes of brightly colored blood as indicators. We found it only a few yards away from where Pops first struck the elk, slanted against a tree on a ridge, dead as a skin rug.

Pink frothy blood seeped out of the wound in its side.

"Must have nailed the lung." Pops said examining the newly opened tear.

My insides twisted a bit, imagining trying to suck in another breath only to have my throat fill with blood instead of air. "What do we do with it now?"

"Help me slide it down to the road; we'll haul it whole in the truck." He said, preferring to bring the carcass to camp and gut it there.

Just below the ridge, there was a dirt path.

I clutched both antlers while Pops grabbed the legs.

We shifted its weight off the tree and began sliding the carcass downhill. My shuffling feet kicked loose soil beneath me. Progressively, we worked our way down at an angle toward the road. Suddenly, a heap of dirt collapsed under my shoes as I lost my grip on the racks.

"Watch it!" Pops hollered.

The elk slid down with the rocks and lifelessly tumbled down like a rag doll, coming to a rolling stop at the foot of the hill, just inches from the path.

We attached the hunting tag to the Elk's head and snapped a few photos together. Despite everything, it felt good being with Pops in that moment, like I'd become a real man in his eyes. That was only a half-truth though — I flubbed it, didn't even take the shot when I had a perfect one lined up. Disappointments are easy to hide behind a smile, but the eyes in a photograph always give it away.

We made it back to camp and brought the truck around, rigged with winches on the headache rack, a few sturdy planks, and a tarp. Stuck to the bumper was a decal of a grey cat's head peeking out from the side, reminiscent of our old cat Cooper, before cancer took him.

It took some manpower, but we finally dragged the bull into the bed. Jesus Christ it was heavy, or *Croist* as Pops always put it.

"Not bad, son," He smiled, scratching his sunburned neck, "not bad at all."

Sweat beaded down both of our faces. It was time to head back.

The trail darkened around us as the sun went down, casting an otherworldly gloom among the trees. I kept looking back from the passenger seat at the elk legs still pointing up, stiffening with rigor mortis.

Without warning, Pops slammed on the brakes. I lurched forward, restrained only by my seat belt. Grit crunched beneath our tires. We were now stationary in the middle of a rocky road on the mountainside.

"What's going on?" I asked.

Pops didn't look over at me. His eyes were fixed on the man kneeling in the ground who had just thrown himself in front of us, all by his lonesome.

"— ease sir I need help!" The man shouted despairingly, both hands over his head like white flags.

A navy blue knit cap rested on his shaggy hair that connected to a dark, scraggly beard. The green outdoor vest he wore gleamed with a reflective substance from the headlights.

Blood.

Pops leaned out his window.

"What is going on here?"

"They shot at us," The man cried and spit some gunk out of his throat. "I don't — I don't know who — they are coming for God's sake!"

"You have to calm down, okay?" Pops spoke back to him,

never losing that stonewall firmness. "Were you shot?"

"No, this ain't my blood. They shot one of my friends, then chased the rest of us. I was separated from the others. Please, sir, they're coming. I just need a ride to the closest station!"

"Dad," I murmured. "He needs help."

His eyes left the man and found me in an empty stare. The sort of look anyone makes when their thoughts get trapped in gridlock. What if the man really was in danger? What if he was lying? Helping a stranger always carried risk, but Pops had a big heart. He would give the shirt off his back if it meant keeping them out of the cold.

"Empty your pockets, first." He told the man solemnly.

"Right, yeah, yes …" The man answered with vigorous nods.

We both watched as he turned his black pockets inside out and unzipped the small pockets on his green vest. He appeared to have nothing on him.

"Hop in the back of the truck, but no funny business. We're armed, you hear?"

"Thank you, oh my god, thank you!" The man gasped.

He limped toward us, more trudging than walking as if he'd never walked a day in his life. Halfway there, he suddenly stopped, lurched forward with a choking sound, and fell to the earth, no longer moving.

Pops popped out of the truck and ran to him.

"Help me get him up."

I hopped out and pulled one of his arms over me while Pops handled the other. The stranger's skin was freezing to the touch and he emitted the worst odor I'd ever smelled in my life. A pungent stench of waste blended with a sweet tinge of cheap, nauseating fragrance settled in my nose. The dead elk was a candle compared to him.

I almost retched as we helped him the rest of the way to the truck.

We should have put him inside the truck bed, made some extra space between the carcass and the planks, but Pops was worried about him. One sore fact I've come to learn about church-going men — sometimes they give too much. He opened the rear door and laid him over the backseat.

We left the interior light on for the rest of the trip. Pop's eyes constantly traveled back to the rearview mirror.

Eventually the man revived again, hoisting himself upright with a wet grunt. His smell was worse in a tight space, even with the windows rolled down.

"What's your name?" Pops asked.

The hitchhiker said nothing, shrinking further into himself.

"Do you know where you're camped at?"

"No." He breathed.

I twisted around and peaked through the small space between the door and my seat. Both the man's grimy hands clung desperately to each other over his black pants, skin so tight I could make out a bulging vein practically popping out of his knuckles. My eyes then wandered to the blood spattered on his clothes. The sight of it made me queasy. Beneath the overhead light, I caught a good look at his face — racing, nervous eyes, clammy skin, and a ragged beard that looked like it belonged to a wet dog.

More homeless than hunter.

"If you want help, you need to work with me." Pops said.

The man cleared his throat.

"We'd been shadowing a herd for a few days," he said. "I heard a gunshot. My friend was on the ground, not moving at all. We thought it was an accident — a misfire from another hunter.

Then more shots came. We ran like bats outta hell. I dropped my gun. You were the first car I saw on the path …"

The truck rolled over a bump in the road.

"So, it was every man for himself." Pops said, his voice carrying a grim tone I rarely heard him use.

The man fell silent, quietly crying into his shoulder. We were approaching a curve along the gravel road ahead of us. I turned back in my seat again and found the chubby vein on the lower part of the man's hand. *Wait,* I thought, *wasn't it on his knuckle before?* In an instant, the bulge began to shiver, spasm, and then slithered up the rest of his cuff like a snake beneath the skin.

I blinked and froze. That wasn't possible, was it? Veins can't do that. Then I realized he was staring directly at me. Two red, bloodshot eyes were now fastened to my own. Neither of us looked away from the other. It felt like he tapped into my thoughts, almost whispering with a silent voice only I could hear —

Did you see it, you little shit?

"Dad!"

I called out instinctively as the truck started into the curve on the dirt path, but when Pops turned his head toward me, the hitchhiker jerked forward. A spray of thick fluid ejected out of his throat and splattered against the windshield in a vile runny coat. I couldn't scream as greenish yellow droplets sprinkled my face and shirt.

Pops yelled an unintelligible curse from behind the wheel as the mucus-like substance thickened over the window like foam in a car wash.

We didn't complete the arc in the road. The tires swerved to the side and went lopsided. The world slanted and then rolled over. For that split second, I felt like I floated. A hellish scream of rattles and gears and rotors striking earth filled the truck as our bodies were thrown left, then right, then up, then down, mere playthings to gravity's unforgiving nature. The window next to me smashed through. Debris of broken glass and globs of the fluid were flying everywhere.

Whatever Pops yelled; I couldn't make out the words before things went dark.

When my vision was clear again, I found myself upside down with intense pressure building up inside my skull. Everything hurt, but the worst pain radiated from my wrist. It was badly bruised and already starting to swell.

Pops was hanging unconscious beside me, his arms limply dangling below him.

"Dad!"

I struggled to call out while tugging at the seat belt squeezing the life out of me. No reassuring voice came from him. Behind us, the hitchhiker had also been upended from the seat, his hat gone and neck slung over. Puss-like threads dripped down his eyes and mouth and formed a cesspool below him, a stench of sickness and rot.

I wrenched the buckle loose and dropped on a pile of broken glass fragments. A few dug into my skin. I dragged myself out through the broken window, trying to avoid any possible pressure on my wrist as I limped to the driver's side. Dark pines surrounded us at the foot of the mountain.

The elk was in an even more grisly state, still attached to the winch by an antler with the rest of its tawny body twisted the other way entirely. Its dislocated jaw hung open and a slimy tongue drooped out. One of our lone planks survived the roll and next to it, bent against a tree, was the white blotch of our cooler.

"Dad, come on, talk to me," I begged, lightly smacking his cheeks, and then focusing on the lap strap holding him up. The seat belt clasp wasn't clicking. Jammed.

I popped open the glove compartment and found the blue pack of our first aid kit and a drop point blade wrapped in a brown leather casing.

A low, guttural growl, followed by a series of slurps, came from the hitchhiker's throat, only growing worse as he convulsed in the back. My eyes were drawn to him. He looked like a body strapped to an upside-down electric chair.

I turned away and sawed madly at Pops' seat belt, trying to cut through polyester without accidentally slicing him in the process. As it finally gave, he tumbled down, almost falling right on top of me. More glass gnashed beneath us as I pulled him out of the truck and back on solid earth. Something else fell from the driver's side as well — The canvas case holding our rifle.

I pressed my ear flat against his chest and felt nothing. Panic erupted through me. I prodded a few fingers in the groove of his neck — Still no trace.

"Fuck, no, no, no."

I panted, quickly lining both hands-on top of one another and compressing his chest. Hot pain circled my wrist and moved up my arm, but I refused to stop.

"Don't do this — Please don't fucking do this, Pops."

I was manic, someplace between blubbering my words and screaming them out.

When I checked again, I found a mild thumping from his heart. Weak, but a heartbeat none the less. It gave me something to cling to with desperate hope. A silent song in a well. A budding seed before the frost.

With my good wrist, I yanked the cell phone out of my pocket. Cracks were scattered all over the screen with a black blotch of dead pixels. I threw it to the ground and screamed at the sky until my voice splintered and my lungs emptied out, crying for someone, anyone, to help us.

What was I going to do? What could I do? I raked through Pops' pockets trying to find his phone. It was nowhere to be found, possibly flung to God knows where. Maybe it was still in the driver's seat, lodged in the sides somewhere?

I twisted towards the overturned truck still spewing out those horrible, throaty sounds.

Then everything fell silent. The gruff rasping had suddenly stopped. Something rustled inside the flipped interior.

Hide, a thought struck me, *you need to hide right now.*

A thump resonated, followed by more shards of glass being crunched. I dove for the canvas rifle case and hid behind the closest tree I could find.

The hitchhiker pulled himself out of the wreckage, his head hanging low and his breathing more haggard than before. He walked with that same clumsy limp as he examined the scene.

More panic swept through me when he noticed Pops on the ground and approached him, looking him over. The sight infuriated me, but I stayed quiet. When finished, he backed up, paced around hastily, and checked the truck inside and out several times. I leaned into the bark and cupped a hand over my mouth. Was he looking for me? Of course he was. I was a loose end; someone who saw something they shouldn't have.

Unable to spot where I'd gone, he returned to Pops and knelt beside him. With a few tormented grunts, he slowly removed his outdoor vest and then pulled his entire shirt off. When I saw his bare spine, I couldn't fathom what I was looking at. Closely packed holes, clusters of them, etched all over his backside, each the size of a tennis ball surrounded by a grim ring of scar tissue. It was like staring at a beehive carved into a spinal column.

With a painful moan, yellowish bile began to ooze out of the hole near his shoulder blade. What looked like a bundle of sticks steadily pushed outward from it. With a sickening *pop*, the object came loose. My hand squeezed my mouth shut as I struggled to contain a terrified scream.

A spider-like thing with ten or twelve skinny legs attached to a bristly skeleton scuttled down from him. Just the sight of it made me want to die.

It didn't stop there. More of these pale, wretched things were wriggling out of the other cavernous holes.

They scuttled busily along the ground before settling on Pops, nine or ten clicking creatures crawling all over him. *No!* the voice inside me screamed. Grayish mandibles tore at his clothes and sank into the skin beneath. *Get away from him!* Small sacks on their pallid bodies grew and inflated red with blood like over-sized ticks.

Get off him you fuckers!

And the hitchhiker, the carrier of these demented things, still hunched over Pops, watching his brood go to work.

Stop, the voice inside me broke, stale as a whimper, *please stop. Please ...*

I covered my ears, but nothing blocked the sounds of their reedy movements. My leg kicked out and bumped the canvas case.

Quiet as I could, I unzipped it and checked on the rifle; despite the hellish rollercoaster it had endured, it wasn't broken. I did the same for the small pouch holding the ammo.

I put the round in exactly as Pops had showed me and slid the bolt back and forth, chambering one. Louder than I wanted, but not giving away my position.

I flipped myself around with the rifle in hand, threading the sight between the stems as I tried to breathe. The hitchhiker was none the wiser, still slumped over with all those weeping holes in his back.

My pulse steadied; my eyes locked on the target. Before I finally pulled the trigger, I visualized the haze of blue particles.

The rifle bucked in my grip as the sound shattered my ear drums. Birds perched up high flew away in a panicked flurry. The hitchhiker did not move, even as the bullet found its mark and tore a brand-new hole in his skull. Around him, spidery things scattered, skittering away from one another like roaches from the light. Most scrambled through the bushes while two raced to the truck.

I chambered another round and fired a second shot toward them. It missed entirely, whizzing past them and into the thicket. I was nowhere near a shot like pops.

Moving cautiously, I approached the hitchhiker, not taking my eyes off him. Blood tinged with drops of yellow bile ran down his neck, threading like a small stream between the fleshy sinkholes of his back until it reached the soupy puddle of wet earth.

When I saw his face, his eyes were still open, staring droopily forward with his mouth left ajar. No sign of life whatsoever.

Suddenly, the twisted Elk in the truck began to squirm as though in the throes of a seizure. It made a sound I'd heard before — a guttural growl only growing louder. It thrashed and convulsed until the final cable holding its antlers came loose, sending it twitching to the ground.

The corpse sprang to life, moving clumsily around like a calf barely learning to walk, its broken neck slung over to the side with its broad tongue flopping about — a nightmare forcing its torn muscles and splintered bones to move like a corrupted piece of clockwork. Flaps of gleaming flesh dangled out of its fur like decomposed tongues.

rrr-RRR-EEEE-UH-UH-uh-uh.

An Elk's bugle, but completely wrong. The screaming call held more of a gurgle and faint cry near the end, like someone blew air through a broken flute and choked on the spit.

Glassy horizontal pupils marked me. With a surprisingly quick gallop, it hurtled in my direction. My legs refused to move. I held up the rifle and centered the scope. The ground around me shook from the stomping hooves. I blew out deeply until my lungs shriveled and as I was about to lose my breath, squeezed the trigger. Nothing happened.

It's not chambered, you need to chamber another round!

Like an ungodly stallion, the elk reared up on its back legs and struck me in the chest with a horny hoof. Hot pain glazed my rib cage. I felt the earth slam against my spine. The elk let out another gurgled screech and descended on me. My mind raced. I instinctively maneuvered left and right to avoid its bone plated feet. They slammed into the ground around me with crazed fury. I clung to the rifle for dear life, keeping it locked in my grip. The jagged antlers swooped for my stomach like a pendulum catching a seam and tore fabric from my jacket in a failed attempt to gut me open.

They ripped through the patch of earth next to my head and swept again just a few inches from my jugular. I would either be gored inside out or trampled into a fleshy clump. It reared the sharp rack again for another disemboweling strike. I punched the bolt into place and then screamed as I jabbed the barrel into its underbelly and fired.

The air pressure shifted against my skin as the crack sent the bullet ripping through flesh and bone. Smoke slid and wafted past its torso as the elk stumbled backward and crumbled into the dirt with a loud thud. Not a muscle moved beneath matted fur. I crawled back in a mad dash away from it.

Was the elk dead? No, it was already dead.

It *had been* dead.

A sudden squelching noise greeted my ears as one of the elk's wounds unfurled like a blooming rose. Two horrifying shapes erupted out of the opening, one managing to scurry into the underbrush while the other spidery-thing dragged its lower half behind it, practically ripped in half by the bullet.

Up this close, the bristly skin looked pasty white and almost human. Its eyeless head fused with its thorax and bared a set of immobile gray mandibles.

Two gangly legs — the ones that were barely attached — were covered in dark boils. Black discoloration traveled down the limbs and over the rest of its abdomen.

A dark pool formed beneath the disintegrating thing as more boils spread from the infected stumps over the rest of its body, sizzling and hissing. The rigid casing composing its skin grew heavy and melted off in thick lumps of tar. The reddened sacks of its back burst like blood blisters. Before long, all that remained of the bloodsucker was a black puddle.

I sat there in shock, staring at the curdling matter.

Voices came, but I couldn't gather my wits enough to understand them. A hand touched my shoulder and made me jump. Some hunters had heard the accident and came to check it out. Help had finally arrived, but it was too late. Pops' pulse never came back.

The church was full for him, and the sounds of tears being shed rang off the walls. His best friend gave the eulogy. Mom smoked outside for most of the service. I don't blame her at all, we were a family of three now reduced to two. We haven't heard much from the *"investigation,"* but I wonder what findings they will choose to keep from us. Straight answers are hard to come by when more departments get involved.

I can still see them, you know, sometimes all over the walls or pockmarked along the floor, small craters ringed with dead flesh and pits too dark to see inside. Clusters. Bundles. All harboring things that shouldn't exist to us. These creatures are following me I think, trying to hide inside me just like the hitchhiker. Was he even alive when we helped him to the car? The answer doesn't matter anymore. The creatures from the holes will not claim me.

I've been working on my aim since then, and I'm a much better shot.

The next time I am faced with my quarry, I will not miss.

Michael Paige has published stories in numerous magazines including The Furious Gazelle, The Scarlet Leaf Review, MetaStellar, Midnight Magazine, Falling Star Magazine, The Horror Zine. *His works have also appeared in anthologies for Savage Realms Press, Crimson Pinnacle Press, Ill-Advised Records, Gravelight Press, October Nights Press, Media Macabre, Little Red Bird Publishing, Chilling Tales for Dark Nights, Culture Cult, Skywatcher Press, Wolfsinger Publication, Jayhenge Publishing, Wicked Shadow Press, Moonday Mag, Eerie River Publishing, Dragon Soul Press, Above The Rain Collective, and Engen Books. Michael resides in Utah.*

VIII

The Angora Incident

By: Mark Gardner

The Angora Incident

Fergus braced himself as the bridge shuddered violently. Alarms blared in his ears.

"Incoming!"

Lynott's warning was barely audible above the deafening crash. A Korsan rail struck the *Sundered Rock.* The ship's frame groaned in protest.

"Evasive maneuvers!"

Fergus' command cut sharply through unfolding chaos, but his voice carried an unmistakable edge of desperation. The ship lurched as Lynott wrestled the controls. Their main view screen flickered, and the Korsan ship stayed dead center despite Lynott's maneuvers. Sparks flew from an overloading console and an acrid smell of ozone filled the air, stinging Fergus' eyes and throat.

"Losing power to port thrusters!" Sweat beaded on Adelaide's forehead, matching her stressed tone. "If they hit us again —"

"Won't get the chance!" Fergus snapped.

While he wouldn't admit it before his crew, Fergus wasn't sure if he fully believed what he said. The ship already groaned under the strain, the old hull screaming. A bone-rattling tremor vibrated through the bridge that made Fergus' stomach lurch. A physical manifestation to match the ship's disintegrating stability.

"Divert everything to engines!" Fergus said. "We need to get out of range now!"

Lynott's eyes flicked between screens, their trajectory showed in moments between attacks.

"Fuel critical, Skipper!" he shouted.

Fergus clenched his jaw; his mind raced while weighing dwindling options.

"Ade, status on the power core!"

"Barely holding," Adelaide replied. "We're lucky that last shot … *whatevered*, but she's not gonna survive another hit." She met Fergus' eyes. "We need to do something — now."

"I think …" Lynott's voice dropped to a murmur. "I think the Korsan ship's core's overloading, I'm … shit, shit, shit …"

A sudden jolt rocked the ship as Lynott pounded on the controls, narrowly avoiding a collision with debris that appeared out of nowhere. The realization hit Fergus hard — they were in trouble.

"Damn it! We're bleeding fuel," Lynott shouted. "If we keep this up, we won't have enough for high-burn!"

Fergus scanned his console, mind whirling. Every option seemed worse than the last. He felt the crew's eyes settling on him, their trust hanging by a thread.

"Ade, watch my engines — if that core goes, we all go," He finally said.

"Already on it!" the engineer replied. "Ready when you are, Skipper!"

"High-burn, now!" Fergus said.

The *Sundered Rock*'s engines roared, pushing the ship's limits. Hull groaning with strain, the sudden acceleration pressed everyone into their seats.

A momentary, unnatural silence filled the bridge, broken only by the hum of the engines and crackling of failing systems. Each crew member held their breath, waiting for their ship to either break free or break apart.

After what seemed like an eternity, the ship leveled out. Alarms resumed shrill cries—a cruel reminder that their ordeal was not over. Damage done, the *Sundered Rock* was a battered wreck, limping through space. Fergus exhaled slowly to steady his breathing, but his sense of dread deepened.

He surveyed the bridge, eyes darting from one crew member to another while absorbing the gravity of their situation. Amber lighting bathed the bridge, casting long shadows against metallic walls. Panels blinked status indicators, displaying the ship's vital signs amidst palpable unease.

They'd been fortunate. The last thing *Sundered Rock* needed was an ambush by a Korsan ship armed with a rail gun. If the Korsan power core hadn't overloaded, that would've been the end. Instead, Fergus seized the opportunity to flee and live to fight another day. Their narrow escape still weighed heavily on his mind as he glanced through the viewport at the scarred hull. How many more close calls could they survive before their luck turned against them and the ship? After a stunned silence gripped him for a few moments, Fergus heaved himself out of his chair.

"Report, people," He cleared his throat while subtly trying to steady his voice. What're we dealing with?"

"Running diagnostics on the core," Adelaide said. "We're lucky it didn't blow us up."

"We're bleeding fuel." Lynott leaned over his controls, muttering as he calculated on a handheld. "Rail gun did a number on us."

"Tungsten plus xenon don't mix." Adelaide cracked a slight, satisfied smile at her own joke.

Fergus preferred better luck than that scenario, but the universe didn't give a damn about what he wanted, and he took the win.

"Can we reach Akbugha with the new fuel profile?"

Lynott's grimace made it clear they were now out of range.

"Find us a rock we can land on for repairs and fuel," Fergus said.

"Aye, Captain." Lynott tapped his display. "We've got options: Ukulan and Shalyk. Ukulan is closer, but it'll add a day to our route. Shalyk is on the way to Akbugha, but it'll be close. Might run out of fuel during re-entry."

Fergus nodded. A delay was preferable to a practical lesson in gravity. He walked to Walker's station.

"Anything worth knowing about Ukulan?"

"Besides the locals hating outsiders?" the first officer replied.

Fergus grunted and shook his head. They didn't have time to worry about baseless rumors. He stared at his crew. Adelaide shrugged. Lynott looked as wide-eyed and apprehensive as Walker. He sighed.

"This isn't a vacation; we're not settling there or mingling with locals," Fergus said. "Just a repair and refuel. Can they do that?"

"Presumably." Walker tapped his console. "Wiki hasn't been updated. Last conglomerate ship sent there disappeared. No atmosphere. Mostly exports. Unless there's a dome breach, we should be okay."

Fergus drew closer to his chair and slapped him on the shoulder.

"Send our client a message explaining our delay. Lynott set

course for Ukulan."

"Course set," Lynott said.

Fergus pointed at his pilot, and the ship soon hurtled toward an uncertain destination.

* * *

Adelaide rummaged through her toolkit. Dim light cast long shadows on the worn metal bulkheads. Her hands moved deftly, familiar with the tools of her trade, but her mind was elsewhere. The *Sundered Rock* had seen better days and so had its crew.

"Ukulan," Lynott scoffed, his gruff voice piercing the silence. He picked up a sheet of metal, examining it with a critical eye. "Whoever named the dwarf planet should've been spaced. Can't be liquid water on more than an eighth of the surface. We've landed at Angora, the only dome with *fuel-cilities*."

He paused, a mischievous glint in his eye. Adelaide ignored his pun and simply cast an unblinking stare at him.

"So, tell me. You know you want to."

"The wiki says it was settled a century ago and thrived," Lynott continued. "Exported real beef to Mars. Can you imagine? Real beef. Terraforming failed, though. Then things … got weird."

He shook his head, a grimace forming on his weathered face.

"No one I've talked to wants to land here a second time."

Adelaide listened intently; her brow furrowed.

"What happened?"

"Officially? COVID-47 about eighty years ago. Wiped out almost everyone under the dome. They never recovered."

"What's the unofficial word?" she asked, thrusting her chin at the hatch to Engineering's narrow passageway.

"The people left are nuts."

"Lynott —"

"Okay, okay." Lynott glanced around, then lowered his voice. "I visited a network forum where freighter crews share information. Walker isn't making it up. Folks from Angora have a reputation for being downright hostile toward strangers."

"And?"

He shrugged. "It's peculiar for a port dome. They want news, you know? Stuff they can't get locally."

"Like contraband?"

Lynott winked. "You'd make a fortune with your homemade hooch."

The atmosphere shifted as Adelaide finished grabbing her tools and they walked to the closed airlock. Tension crackled like static electricity. No one moved. Walker thumbed a button, the sound echoing in the enclosed space as they prepared to breach the exterior. Artificial morning light flooded in, casting harsh shadows on the dock outside. A tall, gangly teenager in gray mechanic's overalls greeted them. His name tag read *C. Ghalib.*

"Welcome to Angora Dome," Ghalib said, his voice tinged with nervous energy. "The quietest docks in the belt. What brings you here when the rest of the system is nicer?"

"Nothing specific," Fergus replied, handing over ship specs. "Just repairs and fuel."

Ghalib glanced at the pad and whistled.

"Those are repairs, all right. Let's get that done and get you on your way."

Adelaide glanced at her shipmates, wondering if they saw something she didn't. Ghalib didn't seem hostile, just... off.

The tall woman behind him gave off a different vibe. She didn't simply scowl at them; she looked… hungry. The way the woman's eyes settled on her made Adelaide's skin crawl.

Ghalib, seemingly sensing her discomfort, glanced over his shoulder.

"Don't mind Leila," he said, his tone light but his eyes flickering with a hint of a warning. "She's good with ships, not people. You'll see when we get to fueling your boat."

"You seem friendly enough."

Adelaide regretted the words as soon as they left her mouth. Fergus frowned at her.

"Sorry, Skipper," she quickly added.

"Heard the locals aren't friendly?" Ghalib's smile faltered. "Yeah, you could say that. I'm from Antalya Dome. Things are… different there. You'll be fine if you don't wander."

Adelaide nodded as a deeper sense of unease settled over her.

"We plan to keep to ourselves as much as possible," Fergus said, his eyes fixed squarely on Adelaide. "Time to get to work."

* * *

Locating the rail's impact was simple enough. Wrenched metal folded into the *Sundered Rock* like shark's teeth. Adelaide's heart raced. Thirty centimeters aft, and the impact would've struck an atmospheric thruster. She shuddered at the thought of the explosion that would've caused. The damage lay beyond her reach, so Ghalib set up a platform for her. Adelaide measured to determine how much material would cover it. Leila watched them for a while, her continuing intense gaze only made Adelaide's skin crawl even worse.

"What brings you to Angora?" Adelaide asked Ghalib once

they were alone. "I mean, if people aren't —"

"Friendly?" Ghalib's laugh was hollow, his eyes darting to Leila, who lingered in the shadows. "It certainly isn't for the local charm. I hoped to join a ship needing a mechanic, but no one's hiring."

"Why not go back to Antalya?" Adelaide asked as she measured a second time, her hands steady amid growing unease.

"I'm saving for a ride off this rock." Ghalib's voice dropping to a whisper. "Angora is the only place on Ukulan that sees any ships these days. Coming here was the worst mistake my family ever made. This planet is dead. In twenty years, there won't be a soul left on Ukulan. The harvest is worse each year, and that famous herd people talk about keeps diminishing. Weirdly, the slaughterhouse here still has plenty of meat."

When he didn't elaborate, Adelaide pushed for a more detailed answer. "Smugglers?"

"Has to be." Ghalib glanced over his shoulder, as if someone might be eavesdropping. "We get ships during local night — more than during daytime — about four or five per week. Don't work the night shift, so can't say for sure. But … you hear things. Strange noises. People talking about things they shouldn't know."

Adelaide applied the patch, her curiosity piqued despite the chill running down her spine.

"What was Angora like when it was booming?"

"Don't know," Ghalib replied, his tone distant. "Been dreary since I got here. You'd have to talk to an old-timer if you can find any that'll talk. Zintan is your best bet but be ready for a long story. He's gotta be a hundred and claims he lived in Angora his whole life. He's reserved when sober. Give him a bottle of whiskey, and he'll talk your ear off."

Adelaide nodded, her mind racing. "Where can I find him?"

"You're serious?" Ghalib raised an eyebrow, his expression a mix of surprise and concern.

"I'm curious."

Ghalib shrugged, though his eyes betrayed a flicker of unease.

"Have it your way." He took a pencil and paper from his pocket and sketched a map of the city. "This is the dock, and over here is the Constable's office. You can usually find Zintan around there. Just avoid southern Angora. The people around here are delightful compared to the people there. Oh, and avoid the slaughterhouse."

Adelaide accepted the map, her fingers brushing against Ghalib's. His hand was cold, despite the dome's warmth. She hefted her toolkit and returned to the *Sundered Rock*, her mind buzzing with questions. Adelaide encountered Fergus outside the lock.

"Hey, Skipper, the patch's done. I'm gonna explore the dome while the *Sundered Rock* gets refueled."

"What?" Fergus recoiled and stared at her like she had lost her mind. "Absolutely not!"

"Aw, come on. Don't you wanna know what's going on here?"

"No. I want to refuel and forget we were ever here."

"Won't be long. I'll have stories to tell. Good ones. Please?"

"Fine. Be back before sundown."

Adelaide suppressed her smirk as Fergus' resolve crumbled.

"Walker's going with you," he added.

"Sir?"

Walker's tone suggested he'd rather clean the bilge.

"You and Lynott put ideas about this place into her head, so one of you goes with her. Lucky for you, you're available."

Both started to protest the arrangement, but Fergus cut them off with a dismissive wave.

"That's how it's gonna be," he said. "No arguments."

Walker fumed and strapped on his sidearm. Adelaide hadn't counted on a chaperone but didn't push her luck. Instead, she kissed Fergus lightly on the cheek before taking her tool bag into the *Sundered Rock*. It was worth seeing the expression on Walker's face.

* * *

Adelaide emerged from the *Sundered Rock* carrying a bottle of brew she made in engineering. She *claimed* it was a solvent for cleaning engine components, but the murky liquid sloshing inside resembled a product from a back-alley distillery.

"What're you bringing *that* for?" Walker eyed the bottle with suspicion. "Getting drunk isn't a good idea."

"Ain't for us," Adelaide replied, her tone light but her eyes sharp. "It's for Zintan."

"Who's Zintan, and why are you trying to kill him?"

"You're just jealous I didn't bring two bottles."

As they walked, Adelaide recounted what Ghalib and Lynott had told her about Angora Dome. The reason for their jaunt became clearer, but Walker still didn't like the idea. Leaving Adelaide without backup bothered him more. Beyond the docks, the dome was nearly deserted. Dilapidated buildings leaned on one another like drunken sentinels, their windows broken or boarded up. The air smelled faintly of decay, though there was no obvious source. They passed a towering hotel with a peeling sign boasting about an award-winning bistro. Lights flickered in upper-story windows, but the grimy door was locked. The occasional Angoran they encountered turned away as they passed, their gaunt, unhappy faces staring at the ground. A few scowled openly but didn't stop long enough to talk.

"They all have face tattoos," Adelaide whispered, her voice barely audible. "Are they ex-cons?"

The tattoos didn't bother Walker. Why should they when he had a wicked scar that ran from his mouth back along his jawline? No, the eerie glint in their hungry, feral eyes got under his skin. They looked at him and Adelaide like they were sizing up a meal.

"Look," Adelaide said, dragging Walker across the street. "That must be him."

A disheveled elderly man shuffled back and forth in front of the Constable's office, rambling nonsense. He passed by them twice before Adelaide grabbed his attention with her brew. He eyed them suspiciously, glanced around, then ambled over to examine their offering. One experimental sniff was all it took. He led them to an alley between the Constable's office and a vacant building. The further from the main street they went, the darker it grew. Walker's hand fell to his sidearm, his fingers brushing the cool metal. At last, Zintan sat on a crate and took a long pull from the bottle. The murky liquid was half gone in an instant.

The old man wiped his chin and cleared his throat.

"Well? This ain't free," he said, his voice raspy and low. "Whaddaya want?"

"Go on, this was your idea." Walker prodded Adelaide as he peered behind crates and refuse. He wasn't sure what he expected to come flying out of them, but his hand was itching to draw his sidearm.

"Can you tell us about Angora?" Adelaide asked, keeping her voice steady amid rising tension. "We're not from here."

"'Course you ain't," Zintan said after another gulp. "No one's from here. You just land here like crap in a bowl. And no one's leaving here alive."

The old man would be the first to go if he kept drinking Adelaide's brew. How was he still conscious? Walker wasn't ashamed to admit that if he or Fergus drank that much, they'd be lucky to *just* pass out. Zintan raised the bottle in a salute and set it beside the crate.

"Don't know why a nice girl like you'd want to hear about a filthy place like this." His voice softened for a moment. "But you gave me a drink, so it's fair payment."

Nice was not how Walker would've described Adelaide, but he held his tongue and got ready for what he assumed would be a load of horse shit.

"See this city?" Zintan began, gesturing vaguely toward the crumbling buildings. "Looks like a trash dump now, but it was plenty shiny at the beginning. Sophisticated. Steaks on every plate. That's what the Martians expected on their way to the Trojans, yeah? Then, the terraforming went sour. A passing body messed with the belt, and ice mining here went belly up. We were starving."

Judging by Leila's appearance, other mechanics back at the docks, and gaunt faces they'd seen on the street, Walker suspected all the denizens of Angora were still malnourished. Starving on a planetoid that exported meat. *No*, he thought, *we don't need to solve this mystery. We need to leave.* He refocused his attention on Zintan's story, hoping to garner enough information to persuade Adelaide to return to the ship at once.

"In walks Captain Ennis," Zintan continued, his voice taking on a bitter edge. "Love him, hate him, you couldn't ignore him. He'd rant about how we needed *new opportunities* instead of leaving this rock or laying down to die." A quick pull from the bottle washed away the scorn in the old man's voice. "Most folks thought he was crazy and ignored him. But he was serious enough to take the *Aequor* toward the outer system. He got back months later; tells us he's made *arrangements* and had a hold full of meat as proof. Ships started arriving every other night, and Angora was the gem of the belt again."

"Swell," Walker said, his tone dripping with sarcasm. "What's the catch?"

Zintan ignored him and glanced at Adelaide.

"Your young man is rude," he said with a distinct gruffness.

"I'm not her —"

"Don't mind him," Adelaide said, taking a seat beside Zintan. Walker didn't know how she could stand the stench. "The city was booming, but something happened?"

Zintan hesitated, his gaze shifting between them.

"What happened is we found out what was really going on with those night flights," he said, lowering his voice to a whisper. "What the *arrangement* was."

Adelaide waited with bated breath, but Walker paced. It was getting darker. They'd been gone longer than planned, and the old man was rambling about ancient history. He would've dragged Adelaide away then and there, but Zintan continued his story.

"People disappeared," Zintan's voice was barely audible now. "One or two at a time, but it wasn't long before every family in Angora was short. It wasn't just here, either. Ranches and farms were found abandoned — and they hadn't gone peacefully, if you get my meaning."

"Smugglers?" Adelaide asked, her voice trembling slightly.

"Slavers," Walker hissed. "Or raiders." The hair on the back of his neck prickled. *Damnation*, they needed to get back to the *Sundered Rock*. "Ade, come on."

Zintan nodded.

"Constable Galip figured that Ennis' *arrangement* was why people were missing," he said, confirming Walker's theory. "Said he had proof that Captain Ennis was supplying slavers. The Constable arrested Ennis, his crew, the dock workers, and the butchers. Folks wanted to hang them, but Galip was pious and believed in Martian justice. He announced they'd wait for the magistrate and have a trial. Frontier justice would've been better."

He picked up the empty bottle and stared at it.

"Don't suppose you have another one of these?"

Adelaide smiled and shook her head. Zintan sighed as he leaned back, his eyes closing. For a moment, Walker thought he'd passed out.

"When Ennis missed the next rendezvous with his *partners*," Zintan said, his eyelids still shut. "They came to see why. Eighty years ago, and I still remember. Korsan ships lit up the night sky. They swarmed the jail and shot anyone in their way. Ennis went free, but the pirates dragged off anyone who objected."

He opened his eyes, put the empty bottle to his lips, then cast it away.

"When the magistrate arrived, people were too scared to speak out against Ennis, so they reported the official story as COVID-47 and incinerated the dead."

"Ennis got away with it?" Adelaide's voice had dropped to a near whisper.

"Oh, no. No, no, no." Zintan's eyes gleamed with a dark

intensity. "See, there was a price for helping Ennis clean house. His *partners* insisted that they needed oversight. *Familial oversight.* Some balked at that, but Captain Ennis took a wife, and others followed his example. She had three babies. The two boys ran things in Angora after Ennis passed. The girl left on a Korsan ship that arrived during the day when she turned eighteen. Ain't been heard from since."

The color drained from Adelaide's face, and her eyes grew wider.

"He let them have one of his *children*? Why haven't you told people the truth?"

"Why do you think?" Zintan's voice grew bitter. "No one believes a drunk. Look at him." He pointed at Walker. "He only believes half of it, and probably not the right half. But you, girl, you believe it. So, I'll tell you something I ain't never told no one before. It ain't what *They* did here that should worry you. It's what they're gonna do elsewhere. You ever hear of the *Mareridt?*"

Adelaide shook her head.

"Nightmare demons," Zintan hissed, his voice dropping to a full whisper. "You ask around the docks for Leila Freitag. Share your rations. She'll tell you. She knows all the stories from Earth."

"Ade, come on," Walker said.

His patience was wearing thin from the start. When Zintan ranted about cannibals, that was the final straw.

Cannibals.

Korsans.

Shit.

Adelaide made a fuss about leaving. Walker almost didn't hear the scuffing of feet. He drew his sidearm and spun, but nothing stood at the alley entrance. Zintan's eyes widened. He stumbled down the alley as Walker dragged Adelaide into the street.

"They've seen us!" Zintan wailed, his voice cracking with fear. "Get to your ship! Tell people! Don't come here. *They're* coming!"

"Zintan! Come with us. Walker, tell him —"

"Shut up and walk," Walker snapped, his grip tightening on Adelaide's arm. "Don't look at anyone. Don't talk."

When a scream emanated from the alley, he walked at a brisk pace, trying not to attract attention. Adelaide hurried after him, cursing under her breath.

Just keep going, he told himself. *Be calm.* But he knew he wouldn't be calm until they got off this miserable rock.

* * *

"You've heard this before," Fergus told Ghalib, his voice tight with frustration. "I don't need two engineers. Can barely afford the one I got. If you pay for passage, we're heading for Akbugha. Lots of opportunities there."

"That won't work for me," Ghalib said, his tone resigned as he ported the final tank. "This job pays shit, and I barely have enough to keep eating."

Fergus glanced at Leila. Her demeanor made her an unsettling figure amid the dimly lit bay. She constantly adjusted her earpiece, tilting her head periodically as if listening to something no one else could hear. When Ghalib signaled, Leila operated the console with familiar deftness, pushing xenon with measured efficiency. The outdated equipment on Angora was painfully slow, and the process seemed to drag on forever.

A thick smell of fuel and ozone filled the air, and flickering lights cast long, shifting shadows across the bay.

The process was nearly complete when Fergus' wayward crew approached. Adelaide trailed after Walker, her face pale and drawn. When she changed direction to speak to Leila, Walker instantly grabbed her by the arm and dragged her toward the ship. Judging by their grim expressions, Fergus guessed they'd experienced firsthand the animosity Ghalib had warned them about.

"Did you have an interesting time?" Fergus asked, his voice dry but his eyes sharp.

"Too interesting," Walker replied, his tone clipped.

"This is an awful place," Adelaide added, shivering.

"Couldn't find any snacks?"

Fergus meant his question as a joke, but neither one cracked a smile. He felt his blood pressure rise, a surge of concern intertwined with dread. He wanted explanations, but whatever they had to say, it was a conversation best saved for later. Leila and Ghalib dragged the hose away, and Adelaide reached up to close the port. The outer hatch hissed closed, sealing them inside.

Fergus activated the 1MC.

"Let's get off this rock," he said.

Wordlessly, Adelaide hustled toward engineering. Fergus followed Walker to the bridge, his mind racing. Lynott waited inside, his console's glow casting eerie shadows across his features. He grinned at Walker, though the expression didn't reach his eyes.

"Have fun?"

Fergus waved him to silence as they finished their preparations. He felt the reassuring rumble of atmospheric thrusters engage, a low vibration reverberating through the ship. For a moment, it felt like they might actually make it out of this cursed place. Then the rumble increased to a deafening roar, topped only when a contaminant klaxon blared, its shrill cry cutting through the air like a knife.

"Set us back down!" Fergus yelled, his voice barely audible over the alarms. He grabbed the 1MC. "Everyone out!"

Lynott was the last to stumble off the bridge after securing the ship. They gathered at the cargo lock, their faces tense and drawn. Adelaide's fingers moved over the controls with practiced ease, her focus unwavering. She might be young — and batshit crazy — but the girl knew what she was doing. Another alarm sounded, and the inner and outer hatches clunked with heavy finality. Fergus fought to get the hatches open, cursing as they jammed halfway.

They rushed down the ramp, boots clanging against the metal. Ghalib met them, eyes wide with concern. He bent his head over a tablet with Adelaide, and an urgent exchange in hushed tones followed. She sprinted off, disappearing into the ship's depths before Fergus could stop her to ask what she was planning. She returned with a pair of gas masks, and the weight of their predicament settled heavily upon them all.

The crew gathered around the ship's perimeter as Adelaide emerged from the still-open hatch. Her face was smeared with grease and soot blackened her hands.

"Debris in the thruster fuel," she said, wiping a dirty hand across her face. "Cut the tank line and pushed gaseous ammonia into our boat. We patched it, but unless we all want to spend the next six hours in masks, we need the scrubbers to take care of it."

Fergus' brow furrowed, his mood darkening with each word.

Fuel debris wasn't uncommon in the belt and beyond, but the timing of this setback ate at his already frayed nerves.

"Nice trick." He rounded on Ghalib, his frustration boiling over. "We can't take you on, so you make sure we can't leave?"

"No!" Ghalib protested, his voice rising. He glanced at Leila, who stood silently in the shadows, her expression unreadable. "We wouldn't do that."

Fergus's frustration stopped him from listening.

"Just leave us to take care of our boat," he said. "We'll camp here overnight and be out of your way at first light."

Walker and Adelaide exchanged glances, and both began to speak. Leila even muttered something under her breath, though her words were lost in the noise.

"The temperature control's lousy," Ghalib said, cutting them all off. "Night crew isn't here yet, and I don't have the key to the office. It'll get below freezing during the night cycle."

Fergus surveyed his weary crew. Two fates awaited them if they stayed with the ship through the night: asphyxiation or hypothermia. Both were equally grim.

"Point taken," he conceded, his voice heavy with resignation. "Let's pack up and find a spot in town before it gets any darker."

"We saw a hotel," Adelaide said, her voice hopeful.

"A crumbling hotel," Walker muttered, his tone dripping with sarcasm.

"Captain?"

Fergus turned, surprised to find Leila standing behind him. She scribbled something on a pad of paper, tore off the top sheet, and handed it over, her expression unreadable in dimming twilight.

"It's our fault you're grounded for the night," she said. "Go to the *Pera Taksim*. Show this to the Oda görevlisi, and you'll get a room for free."

"The *Pera Taksim* isn't as bad as Walker says," Adelaide added, reading the note over Fergus' shoulder. "A bed and a hot shower sound good to me. Maybe the bistro'll be open for dinner."

Fergus nodded, though his gut told him nothing about this place was as it seemed. *We could all do with a hot meal*, he thought. Still, the thought of dinner awaiting them did little to ease the knot of dread tightening in his chest.

* * *

Walker zipped his flight jacket. Worn fabric offered scant protection against the cold of Angoran night. The artificial sun disappeared, leaving the distant glow of Sol splashing across the horizon. He raised a gloved hand and extended his thumb, the gesture futile against the vast expanse of darkened sky, where stars twinkled like distant beacons. A pang of longing swept over him as memories of the Red Planet flooded his mind.

Damn, I miss Mars.

Navigating Angora's labyrinthine streets to reach the Pera Taksim proved harrowing. Sporadic streetlights cast shadows that danced across crumbling buildings, obscuring their path and heightening their unease. Using the flashlight function of their tablets, they stumbled along, relying on Adelaide's map. The city wasn't bustling, but more people were out than earlier, their shadow-obscured silhouettes moving like specters through darkness.

Every person they encountered seemed to bear what Walker considered the *Angora Look* — gaunt, tattooed faces and intense, feral eyes that marked them as survivors in a world relinquishing its humanity. They might not be Korsans yet, but they would be soon if they didn't abandon Angora. They appeared almost otherworldly, their presence unsettling and foreboding. *Zintan's nightmares.* Had some rogue element murdered the old man, or was it a show meant to frighten them away from this place? Walker kept a grip on his sidearm — a comforting reassurance against encroaching darkness. Lynott and Fergus mirrored cautious stances, all eyes scanning the shadows for danger.

The towering *Pera Taksim* façade offered sanctuary amid the desolation. A dozen upper-story windows glowed, and the front door was unlocked. A soft chime overhead signaled their arrival. While they waited, Walker surveyed their surroundings, taking in a once-elegant lobby's faded grandeur. He'd seen pictures of places like this — wood paneling, embroidered upholstery, and velvet curtains. All fallen to decay, colors faded, threads frayed. A portrait hung along one wall, its subject gazing down with a silent, watchful face. The nameplate identified him as Captain Ennis.

A middle-aged man swept into the lobby, crossed to the door, and locked it behind them. His suit, once expensive and tailored, hung on his wasted frame.

"You almost didn't make it," he said. "Lucky for you, I'm behind schedule. So much to do, you see. What brings you to the *Pera Taksim?*"

Fergus handed him the note from Leila.

"Ah," the manager said. "Friends of Leila's. Well, then."

He reached behind the desk and withdrew a ring of metal keys. He sorted them slowly, glancing up at his guests, counting their number, eyeing Adelaide.

"Will the lady want her own room?"

"No," the three men said in unison.

"Indeed," the man in the suit cast a wary glance at Adelaide.

"Is the bistro open?" Adelaide asked.

"The bistro? …" He faltered and paused for a moment before continuing. "Ah, the sign. No miss, I'm sorry, but we've had difficulty filling orders. Perhaps in the morning, I'll have something before you depart."

The man in the suit cleared his throat.

"Suite 2-2, one level up. Housekeeping has been lax. I can't get enough help. Keep the windows closed. It gets frightfully …*cold* … at night."

Fergus led his crew up dimly lit stairs and down a dark corridor to suite 2-2. A musty odor permeated the decrepit room. Any luxury that might've existed faded long ago. A bare bulb swung overhead in place of an ornate chandelier. Dust covered every surface. Lynott and Walker heaved a credenza in front of the door before investigating other rooms.

"Skipper, it ain't five stars," Adelaide said, "But Leila seemed to want to help."

"And we might get a decent sleep before we leave," Fergus said. "Experience has taught me Lady Luck is a fickle mistress. We'll take precautions. Especially not knowing who's staying here. Walker, what do we have out the window?"

Walker drew back a dusty, threadbare curtain.

"One-story drop to an alley. Broken fire escape. Lots of shadows."

Lynott stepped out of a closet, monogrammed linens in his arms.

"The closet is full of this," he said. "Might've been washed a year or two ago. Reminds me of that time when …" he glanced at Adelaide. "Never mind."

"Wait? What? What time?"

"You know how to tie a sheet bend?" A sheet unfurled as Lynott tossed a linen toward Adelaide. He grinned at Fergus. "You thinking what I'm thinking?"

"Let's get practical use out of these linens," Fergus said. "Strip the beds, too. Here's how it's gonna be. Walker and I'll take turns keeping watch. If nothing happens, that'll be it, and we'll laugh about it later. If something does, whoever's on watch will wake everyone quietly. We'll slip out the window. Walker first, then Lynott, then Ade. I'll cover our backs. Once we're down, we head to the dock. I know they said it would be cold, but the night crew needs someplace to stay."

His crew immediately set to work fashioning ropes from the sheets.

* * *

Dawn was still a few hours away when Fergus relieved Walker. Not that he had slept. Both men sat in silence, each consumed by their own thoughts. The room's dim amber light cast long shadows on the walls, and a musty smell of decay permeated the air.

"You never said what happened in town," Fergus said, a yawn slipping out. His voice treaded slightly above a whisper, as if speaking too loudly might summon a phantom from the shadows.

Walker looked away, then yawned himself.

"You didn't ask," he replied, his tone flat.

Fergus frowned. Walker was right—he hadn't asked. He focused solely on getting the *Sundered Rock* off this cursed rock. But now, with the hotel's eerie silence pressing in on them, he couldn't shake off a growing unease. Stories about Korsan raids and feral humans lingered in his mind, gnawing at him like a splinter.

Walker sighed, breaking the silence.

"I think the Korsans were here."

That woke Fergus up.

"What?" he said, his voice sharp. He paused, thinking he heard something in the hall — scraping, like nails dragging across wood. He stiffened, his hand instinctively brushing the hilt of his knife. "Is that what the old man told you?"

"Not exactly." Walker's eyes darted to the door. "Maybe. He was drunk."

Another sound. A low murmur, rising into an unnatural giggle. Then, silence. Fergus and Walker exchanged glances. Palpable tension filled the room, the air thick with an unspoken fear that they weren't alone.

A knock at the door. Polite. Measured.

"Room service," a voice called from the hallway.

Walker's eyes widened. Fergus shook his head. No one had come to check on them all night. He reached for his blade as Walker crept toward the window, preparing their makeshift rope.

Then, the doorknob rattled.

Scratching. More whispers. A child's laugh.

And then —

A wet *thunk* against the door.

Something heavy slid down the wood, leaving a dark smear beneath the threshold. A moment later, an object was pushed under the door. Walker bent down, squinting in dim light. A folded piece of paper, smeared with something black and reeking.

He turned it over. A single word was scrawled in jagged

handwriting:

Hungry.

The door buckled inward as something heavy slammed against it. Hands — too many hands — clawed at the frame, nails splintering the wood. A wet, gurgling sound came from the other side.

"Out the window!" Fergus barked, his voice cutting through the chaos. "Now!"

Walker flung the rope down. Adelaide and Lynott woke, their eyes darting to the door as another sickening crunch echoed through the room. A piece of the door frame cracked and split apart. A single, bloodied hand squeezed through the gap, fingers flexing.

"What the hell is that?!" Panic threaded through Adelaide's voice.

"Move!" Fergus shouted.

Walker was out first, landing in a crouch in the alley below. He immediately took up a defensive position, scanning surrounding shadows for more threats.

"I'm next!" Adelaide said, climbing onto the windowsill.

As she grabbed the rope, a feral human lunged at her from behind. Jagged nails dug into her leg. She screamed, kicking wildly.

"Get it off me!"

Lynott grabbed a broken chair leg and swung it at the creature, smashing its skull with a sickening crunch. The feral human released Adelaide, but more were already climbing over the bed, eyes glowing in the darkness.

"Go, Ade! I'll hold them off!" Lynott said, panting.

Adelaide slid down the rope, landing heavily beside Walker. Blood oozed from deep scratches on her leg. Her face had grown pale with shock.

"You okay?" Walker asked, grabbing her arm.

"Yeah. Just… just go," Adelaide replied, her voice shaky.

With them safely outside the room, Fergus turned his full attention to pushing back the advancing horde. He and Lynott fought back-to-back, using whatever they could find as weapons. Lynott swung the chair leg like a club, while Fergus wielded his knife, slashing at feral humans closing in.

"There's too many of them!" Lynott grunted.

One feral human leapt at Lynott, knocking him to the ground. Jaws snapped inches from his face as he struggled to push the creature off his chest. Fergus stabbed Lynott's attacker in the side, and it let out a gurgling scream before collapsing.

"Get to the window!" Fergus said, grabbing Lynott by the hand.

Lynott scrambled to his feet, but another feral human grabbed him from behind. Teeth sank into his shoulder and he cried out in pain. Fergus lunged forward, driving his knife into the creature's neck. It released Lynott, but the damage was done.

"I'm hit … I'm hit …" Lynott said, clutching his shoulder.

"We're almost out," Fergus said. "Just hold on!"

When they reached the window, a sudden movement caught Fergus' eye. A feral human had climbed in through the broken door and now crouched on the ceiling, head twisted at an unnatural angle. It let out a high-pitched screech and launched itself at Fergus.

"Look out!" Fergus shouted.

He ducked, and the creature sailed past him, crashing into the wall. Lynott grabbed the rope and started to climb down. The feral human recovered quickly and lunged again. This time, it latched onto Lynott's leg, dragging him back into the room.

"Fergus! Help!"

Fergus grabbed the creature by the throat and slammed it against the wall. It twisted in his grip and bit down on his forearm. He let out a pained shout and stabbed the feral human repeatedly until it went limp. Lynott was already halfway out the window, but his injured shoulder made it difficult to maintain a steady grip on the rope.

"Lynott, go!" Fergus said. "I'm right behind you!"

Lynott slid down the rope, landing with a thud in the alley. Fergus followed, but as he reached the bottom, he heard a loud *snap*. The rope had torn. Feral humans now leaned out the window, their eyes glowing in the darkness.

"Hungry ..." one hissed.

The crew didn't stick around to see what would happen next. They bolted down the alley, the sounds of pursuit close behind. Lynott stumbled, his shoulder bleeding heavily, but Walker grabbed him and dragged him along.

"We need to move!" Walker said. "They're right behind us!"

As they ran, Fergus heard feral humans closing in, their guttural growls and laughter echoing through empty streets. The crew stopped and huddled in shadows near the dock, breaths shallow and hearts pounding.

A black mass descended from the sky, blotting out all visible stars. Decrepit ships, barely held together by rust and desperation, breached the atmosphere, landing wherever they found space. The collective roar from their engines filled the air, a deafening cacophony that made the ground tremble. The exhaust was blistering, forcing the crew to press against cold ground, their bodies caught between searing heat above and icy chill below. Atmospheric pressures made Fergus' ears pop as the dome's AI systems struggled to adjust between breaches, the air itself seeming to rebel against the invaders.

Lynott grabbed Fergus' arm, his eyes wide with a mix of fear and disbelief.

"Some of these ships haven't flown in decades," he whispered, his voice barely audible over the din.

"Korsans," Walker spat, voice dripping with contempt. His hand tightened on his sidearm, his knuckles white.

"This could be our chance," Fergus said, keeping his voice low as he scanned the chaotic scene. "Let the Angorans and the Korsans slaughter each other. In the confusion, we can slip aboard the *Sundered Rock*."

Walker's eyes narrowed, his jaw clenched.

"You're out of your mind," he said.

"What about Ghalib and Leila?" Adelaide insisted, her voice trembling. "They tried to help us."

"Since when do you care about anyone besides yourself?" Fergus snapped, letting his frustration boil over. He immediately regretted his tone and took a calming breath. "Look, I'm not convinced they were helping. We barely escaped the Korsans, and now they're landing here."

"It wasn't us."

Eyes widened collectively at hearing another voice. Fergus turned around and saw Leila, half-hidden by shadows, her face streaked with blood and her hand pressed to a wound on her temple. Walker aimed his sidearm at her, his finger hovering over the trigger.

"It wasn't us," she repeated, her voice steady despite her injury. "When the night crew didn't come on duty, we knew something was wrong. Ghalib was at the hotel. He tried to warn you —"

"Don't believe her, Skipper," Walker hissed, his eyes darting between Leila and the surrounding chaos. "She's one of them!"

Leila's glare was fierce, her eyes burning with a mix of anger and desperation.

"I can get you to your ship," she insisted. "Follow me before the Rider gets here with his tribe."

"Too late," Lynott muttered, his voice grim. "It ain't fair."

"What ain't fair?" Walker glanced around the corner, then cursed under his breath. "Those fuckers are in cahoots!"

Fergus peered from their hiding spot. His stomach churned at what he saw. A group of Korsans and Angorans concluded a meeting before moving in different directions.

They'd been set up.

His eyes burned with rage as he turned to Leila. She motioned for him to follow her. Walker and Lynott began to protest, but Fergus silenced them with an icy stare.

"Where's the ship?" he demanded, his voice low and urgent.

Leila glanced toward the docks, her expression unreadable in the dim light.

"They moved it," she said. "It's lower now, hidden. I can take you there."

Fergus hesitated for a moment, weighing the risks. He didn't trust Leila, but now they had no choice. If they wanted to survive the night, they had to follow her.

"Lead the way," he said, his voice tightening with tension like a guitar string.

Leila nodded and slipped into the shadows, her movements almost ghostlike. The crew followed in her footsteps, faces etched with terror as they moved through the chaos, sounds of Korsans and Angorans closing in around them.

* * *

Ghalib joined the group outside a derelict ship, his face pale and his breathing ragged. An acrid smell of burning fuel and the metallic tang of blood choked the air. The surrounding chaos was deafening, with roaring engines and distant Korsan screams blending into a nightmarish cacophony.

"With all those ships out there, it'll be easier to sneak aboard *Sundered Rock*," Walker muttered, barely above a whisper. His eyes darted nervously toward the shadows, where Korsans moved like specters.

Fergus nodded, his jaw clenched. "We won't have to cross open ground."

"They'll have guards on her," Lynott said, his voice tight. He glanced at Adelaide, who was already pulling a gas mask from her toolkit.

Walker gave a curt nod.

"Reconnaissance?"

Fergus pointed his finger at his first officer. "Go."

Walker slipped between two ships, his movements quick and silent, like a shadow in dim light. The others waited, breaths shallow and hearts pounding. Every second felt like an eternity.

"Ade," Fergus whispered, his gaze not straying from the dock, "will the scrubbers be done?"

"Should be," Adelaide replied, her voice steady even with fear swimming in her eyes. "I might need a mask in engineering, though."

He nodded, his mind racing. "We'll need to burn hard to get out of here. How long until we're skids up?"

"The core's hot," she said. "Makes the scrubbers more efficient. We can launch right away."

Fergus turned to Lynott, gripping his arm.

"There could be ships in orbit."

Lynott met his gaze, his expression grim.

"Rail guns, magnetic grapple …"

"They could set off an EMP," Adelaide added.

"That's a lot for one ship," Fergus replied, though his mind was already calculating the risks. "Does hardened protocol add anything to our G-T-F-O?"

Adelaide shook her head.

"Just whacky maneuvers by our hotshot pilot."

Lynott winked and flashed a brief knowing grin.

"Two sentries," Walker whispered, slipping back to the group. "Both armed with shotguns."

Fergus frowned.

"Two? For a fleet that size?"

Walker nodded.

"Plenty of ships for cover, but they're on alert."

Fergus turned and faced Lynott and Adelaide.

"We'll sneak as close to *Sundered Rock* as possible," he said, his voice low and urgent. "Walker and I'll take out the guards. Once those bodies hit the ground, we need to move inside. The shots will likely bring the Korsans back to their ships. Straight to your stations, and we get off this rock."

Lynott and Adelaide both nodded, their faces set with determination. Fergus and Walker crept next to a decaying cargo ship, its metal hull rusting and breached. Through the gaps, they saw guards, shadows shifting in the dim light. Walker gave a hand signal, and the two men burst through the cargo ship and out the other side.

Two shots rang out, echoing in the still night. Fergus slapped his palm on a panel next to the auxiliary lock, and the door hissed open. Lynott and Adelaide sprinted from cover, slipping inside the opening lock. Fergus and Walker piled in after them, and Walker slapped the controls inside the lock, sealing them in the ship.

"Sequence the main hatch," Fergus said, glancing over his shoulder as he sprinted toward the bridge.

Lynott dropped into the pilot's chair, reached under his console, and flipped a switch. Fergus' status board lit multiple green indicators—more than there should be. The ship rumbled, engines roaring to life.

A loud thud came from the corridor. Then another. Heavy footfalls, stumbling, dragging. Walker spun, weapon half-raised, just as Leila and Ghalib staggered onto the bridge.

Leila was pale, a dark stain spreading down her pant leg. Ghalib barely kept her upright, his face slick with sweat.

"What are you doing here?" Fergus demanded, his hand hovering over his sidearm.

"The Korsans are swarming the docks," Leila panted, her voice tight with pain. "Ghalib helped me to the ship, but we didn't know if we'd make it."

"They came out of nowhere," Ghalib added, breathless. "She got hit. I wasn't leaving her behind."

Adelaide stepped forward, casting Fergus a glance.

"She needs help, Skipper," the engineer said. "We can't just throw them out."

Fergus' jaw tightened. He didn't trust them, but Leila's injury wasn't fake. He glanced at Lynott, who gave a small nod. Time was running out.

"You're with us," Fergus said at last. "Leila, get to aux; Ghalib, help Ade in engineering."

They nodded and ran down the corridor, Ghalib half-carrying Leila.

Fergus glared at the stubborn status board. The ship shook, alarms blaring across the bridge.

Fergus cursed under his breath. "Lynott, get us in the air, now! We'll deal with them in the sky."

"Aye, Skipper!"

The *Sundered Rock* lifted off the ground, dust and debris swirling. The dome's cracked surface loomed closer, offering a grim reminder of the horrors they were leaving behind.

"Skipper, the Korsans are moving to intercept!" Lynott glanced away from his console. "They're coming in hot."

"Walker," Fergus hissed. "Report."

"Ghalib and Ade secured the hatch."

"Good. Lynott, steep escape angle. We need to clear that dome and the Korsans."

"Steep escape angle, aye," Lynott said.

The *Sundered Rock* shot upward, engines roaring in the low atmosphere. The Korsan ship was closing in, its hull gleaming ominously in dim light.

"Ade, I need everything you've got from the engines!"

"Already giving all she's got!" Adelaide's voice crackled back.

The ship jolted as it broke through the dome, the structure below shrinking rapidly. Above them, the Korsan ship descended, weapons glowing with malevolent energy.

"Lynott, we need to stay out of their firing arc," Fergus said.

The *Sundered Rock* veered hard to starboard, the sudden maneuver throwing the crew against their restraints.

"They're not giving up!" Lynott said. "They're faster than us!"

Fergus's jaw clenched.

"We'll use that against them. Prepare a turn and burn."

Lynott's eyes widened.

"Spinning her around, Skipper."

The *Sundered Rock* rolled into a tight loop, bringing it on the same plane as the Korsan ship.

"Ade, brace yourself!" Fergus said. "Now, Lynott! Burn!"

Lynott slammed the controls forward. The *Sundered Rock* flipped, bringing its aft toward their pursuer. A plume of superheated plasma erupted from the ship's engines straight into the Korsan bow.

Plasma washed over the enemy vessel. The Korsan ship's hull glowed red-hot as superheated gases tore through metal. It lurched and the ship's descent turned into a slow, uncontrolled tumble as it lost power.

Lynott pumped his fist.

"Direct hit!"

"Get us outta here," Fergus said. "They'll send reinforcements."

"Punching it, Skipper!"

The *Sundered Rock* broke free from the planetoid's atmosphere as the disabled Korsan ship tumbled into Ukulan. Silence swept over the bridge. Fergus found it eerily familiar to the last time they tangled with the Korsans.

Was that only yesterday?

Lynott's voice broke the silence. "Telemetry says knock one."

Fergus nodded and a grim satisfaction settled over him as the *Sundered Rock* sailed into the black sea of infinity.

Mark Gardner is a U.S. Navy veteran living in northern Arizona with his wife, three children, and spoiled dogs. With multiple degrees under his belt, he works in post-secondary education, where he is passionate about fostering learning and growth. Mark's diverse experiences inform his writing, infusing his stories with authenticity and depth.

Also by John Coon

Check out the terrifying *Deer Falls Horror Series* by John Coon from Samak Press. Available in print and eBook editions at booksellers worldwide.

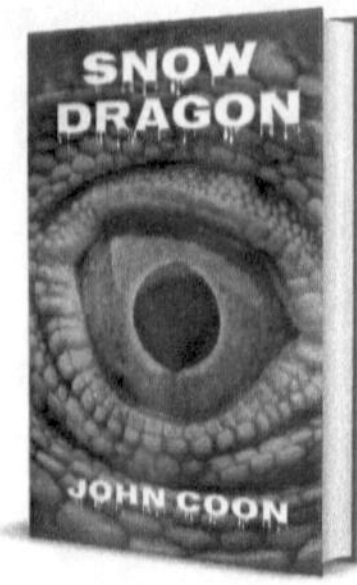

Snow Dragon

A mythical monster has awakened beneath Deer Falls following a major earthquake. Can the Duggan family destroy this vicious and lethal predator before it drives their sleepy Colorado town to extinction?

A prequel novella to the Deer Falls horror series.

Pandora Reborn

A buried chest is unearthed and opened, bringing forth an ancient witch who terrorizes Deer Falls. Will Ron Olson and his new friends stop her before she destroys them and the small Colorado town?

Book no. 1 in the Deer Falls horror series.

The Crimson Reaper

Consumed by a thirst to unlock powerful dark magic, a sadistic killer stalks Deer Falls. Can Eric Olson overcome past trauma to save himself and the rest of the town from destruction?

Book no. 2 in the Deer Falls horror series.